NANTUCKET NEWS

PAMELA M KELLEY

PIPING PLOVER PRESS

ISBN paperback, 978-1-953060-25-9

Cover design by Shaela Kay, Blue Water Books

Thank you to Jane and Taylor Barbagallo, Amy Petrowich and Laura
Horah

Are you on my mailing list? Please sign up for notifications of new
releases and special giveaways.

INTRODUCTION

Charleston native, Taylor Abbott, has just relocated to Nantucket for her dream job as a junior news reporter at the local paper. Ten years ago she was Abby Hodges college roommate and is looking forward to living near her best friend again.

Until her rental cottage is available, she's going to stay at The Beach Plum Cove Inn, Abby's mother's bed and breakfast.

Abby meanwhile is dealing with an issue she thought she'd resolved.

Rhett discovers someone that works for him is a thief and tries to figure out who it is.

Rumor is there's a celebrity or two on the island and the media (including Taylor's co-worker, Victoria), is in hot pursuit to track them down.

CHAPTER 1

"Do we have someone famous dining with us tonight?" Rhett leaned against the hostess stand and glanced at their reservations page for the night. He didn't see any familiar names. But a few of their regulars who were having a drink at the bar while they waited for their table mentioned seeing two television vans outside.

Nantucket didn't have a television station, so they were from off-island, which usually meant they knew there were celebrities there. Could they be in his restaurant? If they were, Rhett wanted them to be able to dine in peace.

Elsa, the pretty blonde hostess, was a young college student working at Rhett's restaurant for the summer. She was friendly and quite good at the job, but she was also easily intimidated, and she looked nervous as she considered Rhett's question.

"I didn't notice anyone. Not at first. But I saw the

vans outside too, as people have been coming in and I've been trying to figure out who it might be. I think it could be that couple in the corner. She looks a bit like Cami Carmichael, the actress, though her hair is darker. I saw on Instagram that she might be filming something here."

Rhett was familiar with the actress and glanced over at the table Elsa indicated. He couldn't really tell if it was her, though. He debated what to do, if anything—but then the girl laughed and smiled, and he knew. Her smile was famous, impossible to mistake.

"I'll take care of it." An idea came to him as he walked over to the table. The young couple looked up, and he recognized Nick Whitley, who was a chef at The Whitley Hotel.

"Hi Nick." He nodded at his companion. "I hope you both enjoyed your dinners?" Their plates were bare, which was a good indication that they had.

"Everything was great. Bella loved the scallops."

That name threw him. But then Bella smiled and Rhett realized it was likely her real name.

"I'm glad to hear it. I wanted to give you a heads up that there are some media people out front." He hesitated, hoping he wasn't wrong about this. But Bella's reaction confirmed it. Her face lost color.

"I didn't think anyone knew we were here," she said.

Nick's irritation was evident. "I have no idea how they found us. They must have followed us here, and we didn't realize it."

Rhett took his keys out of his pocket and removed the

one to his truck and set it on the table. "So, here's what we're going to do. When you're ready to leave, tell Amy, your server, to come find me. Take that key and go through the kitchen and out the back door and drive my blue truck home. I can get it back from you tomorrow. I'll go out front and distract the news folks....they'll have no idea."

Bella looked relieved. "Thank you so much. I think that will work."

"Rhett, I seriously owe you one," Nick said. "I'll drop your truck off tomorrow morning."

Rhett smiled. "I'm not worried about it."

RHETT LEFT THE RESTAURANT AT A FEW MINUTES PAST eleven. His wife, Lisa, was waiting in her car. She'd chuckled when he asked if she wouldn't mind picking him up.

"Of course. Did your car die?"

"Not exactly. I'll tell you on the way home. It's a good story."

And as soon as he hopped in the car and Lisa headed home, he filled her in.

"Cami Carmichael. The girls and I love her movies. Is she as pretty in person?" Rhett wasn't surprised to hear that they were all fans.

"She's very cute. I didn't recognize her right away though as her hair is dark brown now and she was wearing sunglasses."

"Sunglasses inside. Hmm. How did you know it was her?"

"I wasn't sure. Especially when Nick called her Bella. But then she smiled, and it was obvious."

"That's so exciting. And your plan worked, obviously."

"Yes. I went out and talked to the reporters. I asked them why they were there and who they worked for. I asked as many questions as I could think of to buy Nick and Bella some time. I had to laugh, though. They stayed for almost two more hours, before realizing they'd missed her."

"Good. I can't wait to tell the girls at breakfast tomorrow." Lisa's daughters, Kate, Kristen and Abby, joined their mother for breakfast every Saturday at the home they grew up in, which was now a bed-and-breakfast. Rhett was very happy about that as it was how he and Lisa met. He was her first guest and stayed for months while he was getting his new restaurant ready to open. And then he and Lisa started dating and eventually got married. Lisa liked to tease him that he was the guest that came and never left. It was true, and he couldn't be happier about it.

This was his second marriage. He'd been divorced for ten years and had thrown himself into his work, which consisted of several restaurants, which he oversaw with the help of good managers. Getting into a serious relationship was something he didn't think would happen again for him. The Nantucket restaurant, which was simply called Rhett's, was his main focus.

"Was it busy tonight?" Lisa asked.

"Yes. It started early, and didn't let up until a little after nine. It's been like this every night for the past few weeks. Which is great, but I was looking over our books this morning and something seemed off."

"Off how?"

"With the volume of people I'm seeing coming into the restaurant each night, the sales don't seem to always reflect it. The numbers seem a little off. Down somehow and I can't quite figure it out."

"Could it be a mistake of some kind?"

"It's possible. Or it could be that someone has found a way to skim some extra money for themselves."

"You don't really think that, do you? Who would do that?" Lisa sounded shocked at the idea.

"I don't know. I can't imagine anyone that works for me deliberately stealing, but you never know. It's a big problem with restaurants. Not as much now that things are so computerized. It was easier back in the days of handwritten orders. But, something is up and I need to get to the bottom of it."

"I CAN'T BELIEVE RHETT MET CAMI CARMICHAEL!" LISA'S youngest daughter, Abby, said as Rhett brought his cup of black coffee to the table. Lisa had just finished sharing the details of Rhett's evening at the restaurant. All of her girls were already there. Kate, her oldest, was by herself for a change. She was planning to go grocery shopping and run some errands after breakfast, so her twins were home with her husband, Jack.

Kristen, her middle one, had no children and wasn't married yet, but she was in a serious relationship with her next-door neighbor, Tyler. Abby was also by herself for a change, and was planning to join Kate for some shopping before heading home.

Abby was the one that was always interested in celebrity gossip. Not that there was ever much of that on Nantucket, but now and then there were famous visitors to the island and sometimes movies were filmed. There was also the Nantucket Film Festival, which grew every year so that now it was a week or so of various events.

"Rhett, what was she like?" Abby asked. Lisa smiled as everyone waited eagerly for Rhett to speak.

"She seemed nice enough. Said she liked the scallops. So she has good taste." He grinned. "We spoke for all of about two seconds. As soon as I told them there were media vans outside, she went as white as a ghost. The poor kid. They managed to get out of there without being seen though."

"Thanks to you," Lisa said. It was so like Rhett to help out like that. Nick Whitley had already come by just before breakfast to return Rhett's truck and left a box of freshly made cinnamon rolls as a thank you. They were all eating them now with their coffee and they were delicious.

"It was nothing. I was happy to help." Rhett took a sip of his coffee. He always had a full cup before eating anything. "I really can't imagine living like that. With people following you around everywhere."

"Bella managed to stay on Nantucket for a few months undetected," Abby said. "She stayed undercover at The Whitley, and that's where she met Nick. Though I think if I'd run into her, I would have recognized her."

"I almost couldn't tell it was her with the dark hair and sunglasses. It was the smile that gave it away," Rhett said.

"I guess the rumor is true, then. It's been speculated that she was going to start filming a new movie here," Abby said.

"I guess we'll see more of those vans around, then. Especially if there are other famous people here filming, too," Rhett said. He frowned at the thought. "I hope they know better than to come back to my restaurant."

Lisa chuckled. "Well, if they do, you'll know how to handle them."

"True."

"Speaking of the media, Abby, Taylor is checking in today. I'm putting her in your old room." When Lisa converted her waterfront home into a bed-and-breakfast, her son Chase, who was a builder, put in a dividing wall between the downstairs area and the bedrooms upstairs, which was where her children had all slept once. There was also a guest bedroom, and all rooms had their own bathrooms, so it worked well for a bed-and-breakfast.

In the morning, guests could come downstairs and access the dining area where Lisa always set out coffee, juice, bagels and a few hot items like quiche or scrambled eggs.

"How is Taylor? I haven't seen her in years. And why is she staying here?" Kate asked. Taylor was Abby's college roommate.

"Taylor's great. I haven't seen her in a few years either. She was working down south at a newspaper in Charleston. We talk all the time though and when I heard about an opening at the newspaper here, I let her know about it."

Kate looked confused. "If she was working in a bigger city, why would she want to come here? It almost seems like a step backward."

"It's not. She had a small role at a big paper, and only gets to write up weddings, birth announcements and obituaries. Here she can do a lot more." Abby grinned. "And I may have sold her hard on how awesome Nantucket is."

Kristen smiled. "She's been here to visit you before, too?"

"She has, a few times over the years, and she loved it. She has a rental lined up, but it's not available for about six weeks, so Mom is giving her the family and friends discount. I offered to have her stay with me, but she knows we really don't have the room, and insisted on renting until she can get into her own place."

"She'll be right at home here. I'll make sure of it," Lisa said. She enjoyed mothering her kids and their friends. Running the bed-and-breakfast really suited her, as she loved taking care of people and feeding them well.

"When does she start at the paper?" Kristen asked.

"Right away, I think. A day or two after she gets here," Abby said.

"She's not going to be one of those people, is she?" Rhett asked.

"What do you mean, honey?" Lisa asked. The rest of them looked at him in confusion.

"I mean, like those people in the vans outside the restaurant. Is that what your friend is going to do?"

"Taylor? No. Absolutely not. Not following people around," Abby said. At least I don't think so. I think that's just the TV people."

"Good. I'd hate to see a friend of yours doing something like that." Rhett refilled his coffee cup and then reached for the last cinnamon roll. "These sure do look good."

CHAPTER 2

"If you get sick of Nantucket, you can always come to Vermont. We have newspapers up here too."

Taylor smiled as she chatted with her father. She'd just spent a week with him in central Vermont, in the tiny rural town that he'd retired to. It was a beautiful area, but there wasn't much happening there. He liked it that way though and was content to hike his fields and feed his chickens.

Taylor was happy to visit when she could, and now that she was in New England, she'd be able to get away and see him more often than she had living in Charleston.

"I'll keep that in mind, Dad. You should come for a visit once I'm settled in. Have you ever been to Nantucket?"

"No. I went to Martha's Vineyard a few years ago. That was nice. And on the way home, we stopped in Plymouth and visited the Mayflower and Plymouth Rock.

I just read a book about the Mayflower. It's fascinating stuff."

"I'm sure it is." Her father was a big reader, especially of history. "When you come here, we can go to the Whaling Museum. You'll love that."

"That sounds good. Are you there yet?"

"Almost, we should be docking in a few minutes I think."

"Okay, I'll let you go then. I'll talk to you in a few days."

Taylor ended the call and went outside on the deck of the Steamship Authority's car ferry. It was a slower way to get to Nantucket, a little over two hours instead of the hour it would take on the passenger only ferry, but Taylor wanted to have her car with her. She'd driven it from Charleston to Vermont and then through Boston to Cape Cod. She knew she could probably get by without a car on Nantucket, but it was more convenient to have one. An older model Honda Civic, her car was the longest and most reliable relationship that she'd had.

She was excited and a little nervous as she saw Nantucket wharf straight ahead. This was a big move for her. The only person she knew on Nantucket was her former college roommate, Abby. She'd briefly met the rest of her family when she visited Abby a few times, so she supposed she knew them too, but really only as acquaintances. It felt like the right decision, though. She had loved the charm of Nantucket when she'd visited Abby and the opportunity at the newspaper came at just the right time.

Her mother thought she was a little crazy to take the job, though. When her parents divorced, soon after Taylor graduated from college, her father had moved to Vermont and her mother and Taylor stayed in Charleston. Her mother remarried a year later, to the owner of the real estate firm her mother worked at for as long as Taylor could remember. Her mother lived and breathed real estate and Richard, her husband, was the same, so they were well suited.

But Taylor couldn't be more different. Her mother won sales awards every year and was one of the top realtors in Charleston. And she dressed the part and was active in all the best society organizations. She urged Taylor to follow in her footsteps, to at least join the Junior League, but Taylor had no interest. One of the things that attracted her to Nantucket was that it was more laid back and a more natural, less makeup look was the norm instead of the exception.

When she was younger, Taylor used to love chatting with her mother as she 'put on her face', all the layers of foundation and powder, eyeshadow, and sculpting creams. The few attempts Taylor made to do the same had resulted in frustration and melting makeup streaks. She preferred a more minimal approach, a slick of mascara and lipstick, maybe a hint of blush, if that.

Her mother was intrigued, though, by Nantucket real estate. "Honey, that's one of the hottest markets in the country. If you could get into a good office there, you could make a fortune. I'm sure I know someone that could get you an interview." Her mother never understood that Taylor wasn't driven to succeed in the same way. As long as she had enough money to pay her bills, she was fine, and no one went into journalism for the salary.

It had taken her a while to figure out what she wanted to do, though. She'd majored in English and Communications and knew that she wanted to do some kind of job that involved writing. She didn't focus on journalism initially, as she thought something creative might be more fun, maybe in marketing or advertising. Her mother had approved of that, especially advertising, as it was a more glamorous field and if one went into the sales side, the income could be quite lucrative. But sales had never interested Taylor. Her first job out of college was for the biggest advertising agency in Charleston, as an assistant.

She enjoyed the role, even though it was more administrative than anything else-as many entry-level roles are. She made some great friends there, as every year a new batch of recent grads were hired. Some of her friends went onto the sales side while Taylor stayed in creative and was promoted into a junior copywriter and editor role. She edited copy and contributed ideas to new campaigns.

It was fun, at first. But it was also stressful too as there was always a lot of pressure for each new campaign to outperform the last one, and when the results weren't there, they sometimes lost accounts as clients left to go to a new agency. And that often meant layoffs, and it was usually the creative side that took the hit.

Taylor managed to stay there for almost seven years

before getting 'whacked' as they put it, when the agency lost its biggest client.

It seemed like fate though, as she'd been updating her resume and trying to decide what to try next. The layoff gave her the push she needed and two weeks later, she was hired by the newspaper for the community news role, which was basically writing obituaries, wedding and birth announcements. It was a good way for her to experience something new and she quickly felt like she was where she was supposed to be—but not in the right role, yet.

It didn't take her long to learn the duties of the position and she was eager to take on more, to start doing some actual news stories. But she had to get in line for that as the paper was fully staffed and turnover was low, so there wasn't an opportunity to do more than an occasional story when no one else was available.

It gave her enough of a taste that she wanted more, and she grew resentful of the repetitive nature of the wedding and birth announcements. She wanted to move away from that entirely. So, when Abby mentioned the opening at the Nantucket paper, it seemed once again like a sign.

As soon as she emailed in her resume, things moved quickly. Taylor did a Zoom interview with Blake Ojala, the managing director of the paper. She'd been surprised when she did her pre-interview research to see that he was only thirty-six, just six years older than Taylor. His father had started the paper and was still involved as chairman, but Blake had moved into the managing director role a few years ago and handled all the day-to-day running of the paper.

She'd liked him immediately and couldn't help notice that he had a very Nantucket look about him, with his slightly long dark blond hair, and the pale blue button-down shirt and a Nantucket Red baseball hat sitting on his desk. He'd obviously just taken it off for the call, as his hair was a bit mussed. It kind of gave him a preppy surfer look, which she found appealing.

But she'd forced herself to focus on the interview and he'd quickly put her at ease. She knew it helped that he was friends with Abby's husband Jeff, at least to get the interview. Abby had told her, though, that he'd had a lot of applicants, so she didn't get her hopes up and kept sending out resumes. But then the call came with the offer and Taylor immediately accepted.

Finding housing, however, was harder than she'd anticipated. Rents were high on Nantucket, especially for seasonal rentals, which were the majority of what was available. Year-round rentals were much harder to come by and the few that were available were way out of her price range. She'd hoped to have her own place, but that was looking less likely and she started looking at listings for people that needed roommates.

But then, Abby once again came through, or rather, her brother Chase did. He worked in construction and knew someone that had a small cottage that was coming available in two months. She could have it if she wanted it, but would need to find a place to stay in the meantime. He warned her that the cottage was tiny, barely six hundred square feet, but it had everything she needed, including a very distant ocean view from the second floor. There was one bedroom and bath upstairs and a small kitchen and living area on the first floor. When he sent her the pictures by email, she fell in love instantly as the cottage also had a white picket fence covered in bright pink beach roses.

Abby also offered for her to stay with them until her cottage was available, but Taylor knew there was really no room for her there. Plus, she had some money saved, enough to stay at Abby's mother's bed-and-breakfast. She was looking forward to that actually as it would feel a bit like being on vacation as The Beach Plum Cove Inn was beautiful and right on the ocean. She could walk along the beach whenever she wanted a little exercise, and it was just a few miles from Abby and the newspaper.

Taylor put the address in her GPS as she waited in her car for her turn to drive off the boat. She enjoyed seeing the old cobblestone streets downtown and all the tourists walking around. It was a beautiful, sunny day. Warm for mid-March. Vermont had been blanketed with snow while Taylor visited, and there wasn't a sign of the white stuff on Nantucket. She hoped it stayed that way. Although it was fun to see an occasional flurry. That rarely happened in Charleston.

It didn't take her long to reach The Beach Plum Cove Inn. She felt a thrill as she pulled into the driveway and caught a glimpse of the ocean behind the house. The sunlight glimmered on the water and the beach beckoned her. Once she was settled in, she'd go for a nice walk to stretch her legs and explore.

There was a lighthouse not too far off—maybe she could walk down and back. She was grateful for the timing too, as she never could have afforded to stay here in the summer when the rates were the highest. But now, in the off-season and with the friends and family discount, it was manageable. She parked her car, grabbed her suitcase, and headed to the front door to check in.

CHAPTER 3

"What can I bring tonight?"

Lisa thought about her friend Marley's question as she gave the veal Osso Buco a stir before closing the slow cooker lid. It had already simmered for a few hours, smelled heavenly and by the time the girls arrived around six, it would be falling off the bone delicious.

"Maybe just a bottle of wine, whatever you feel like drinking. Paige is bringing a salad and Sue is bringing brownies for dessert," Lisa said as she settled back onto the stool at the kitchen island and pulled up her Shopify account to see the day's orders, as she knew what Marley's next question would be.

"How are sales?" Marley had an e-commerce background and she and Lisa became good friends when Marley stayed at the inn for a while after her divorce. Now she lived year-round on Nantucket and had a thriving digital marketing consulting business, and Lisa was her first client.

"They're still really good."

Marley laughed. "You sound so surprised. I told you this would happen. If you have a great product and market it well, good things happen and word-of-mouth kicks in. Your lobster quiche is to-die for."

When Lisa ran into an issue with not having a license to serve food—something she hadn't realized she needed for the hot breakfast items she served to her guests—they came up with a solution. Rhett helped her to design a commercial kitchen addition that her son Chase built, and then Marley oversaw a website to sell her quiches and other items online.

Lisa had no idea what a big business online food sales could be. But she was pleasantly surprised as every week, sales grew and she'd had to hire help to staff the kitchen and make the items. She was having a lot of fun with it though.

"I was surprised. Every day when I check the numbers, I always expect to see that sales are down, but they almost never are. Rhett turned on a feature that plays a cash register sound whenever there's a sale and that was so fun at first. I laughed every time I heard the sound."

"I bet you have that turned off now, though? The thrill wore off fast."

"Yes. It's off now." Lisa glanced out the window and saw a silver Honda pull into the driveway. "I think my newest guest has just arrived."

"I'll let you go. See you tonight. I'll bring some kind of red—whatever Peter recommends." Peter Bradford owned the local liquor store and was also dating Lisa's friend Paige.

"Perfect. Tell him I said hello." Lisa ended the call and a moment later, the front doorbell rang.

She opened the door and smiled. As expected, her new guest had just arrived. Lisa had met Taylor Abbott several times when she'd visited Abby on summer breaks. She was a pretty girl, a little on the short side, with dark brown hair that fell in a long, shiny bob to her shoulders. Her eyes were just as dark and were the first thing you noticed about her face. That and her warm smile. She also looked exhausted.

"Taylor, so nice to see you again. Come on in. Would you like a hot cup of tea or coffee? I was just about to make one. You must be tired from your trip."

"I'd love a cup of tea if it's not too much trouble. After that, I think I need a hot shower and either a nap or a walk on the beach to wake up. I'm not sure."

Lisa laughed. "I'd save the walk for tomorrow. Relax and rest up today. How long was your trip?"

"I was visiting my father in central Vermont, so a little over five hours to get to the Cape and then a few more hours on the ferry."

"That is a long day," Lisa said as she put a kettle on the stove to heat up some water. "While it's heating up, I'll give you a quick tour and show you to your room. You can drop your suitcase off."

She showed Taylor the commercial kitchen first, since they were right there.

"Abby told me about the online store. That's so exciting," Taylor said.

"It has been fun," Lisa admitted. She walked into the dining room next. "This is where you can come for breakfast anytime between eight and ten. There's always coffee and juice, bagels or toast and fruit and a hot item or two —it varies by day."

"That sounds wonderful."

Lisa took her upstairs next to room number three, which faced the ocean. "This was Abby's room. It's slow right now. I only have two other rooms rented, and one of them is leaving tomorrow. So, it should be nice and peaceful for you."

Taylor set her suitcase in a corner and walked to the window. In the distance, they could see another ferry arriving. "I think I might just stare out this window all the time. The view is amazing."

Lisa smiled. "Thank you. We love it here. I think the water should be ready for tea now."

They headed back to the kitchen and Lisa poured two cups of tea and they sat at the island. She put out a bakery box of chocolate chip cookies. "You need to try one of these. Kate dropped them off from a new bakery in town and they're so good."

"I had lunch on the boat, so I'm really not hungry," Taylor said. And then grinned. "But these do look amazing." She reached for one, took a bite, and swooned. Lisa laughed and reached for one, too.

"So, when do you start the new job?" Lisa asked.

"The day after tomorrow. So, I have all day tomorrow to explore. I think Abby is having me over for dinner tomorrow night, so that should be fun."

"Good. You also have a small fridge in your room and a microwave, so you can pick up a few things at Stop and Shop and make sandwiches or heat up soup, whatever you like. Tonight, if you don't feel like going out, there are a few local places, pizza, Thai and so on that deliver. There's a list in your room with their phone numbers."

"Oh, that's perfect. Thank you." Taylor's eyes were starting to look heavy. Lisa could see that the long trip had caught up to her.

"If you need anything, my number is on that sheet, too. Don't hesitate to call. Otherwise, hopefully I will see you at breakfast in the morning?"

Taylor finished her cookie, took a final sip of her tea, and stood up.

"Thanks again, for everything. I will definitely see you in the morning."

Lisa walked her to the front door and as she opened it, remembered something Abby had said at breakfast.

"Abby mentioned that another new girl just started at the newspaper too, just this last week. Abby thinks that she's about your age, so that should be fun for you."

Taylor looked surprised. "Really? That's interesting. I didn't realize there were two openings."

"I'm sure Abby can fill you in tomorrow when you see her."

MARLEY TOOK A BITE OF LISA'S VEAL OSSO BUCO AND sighed. The meat was so tender and the rich sauce silky smooth and so flavorful with lots of fragrant mushrooms. Lisa served it over a big mound of whipped potatoes with sautéed spinach on the side.

"Lisa, this is amazing, as usual. And Paige, Peter was so right about this wine. It goes perfectly with it." When she'd stopped by Bradford's liquors and told Peter what they were having, he instantly recommended a wine that Marley wasn't familiar with, an Italian Amarone.

Everyone agreed that both the wine and veal were delicious, and they laughed and caught up with each other as they ate. Marley knew that Paige and Sue had been Lisa's best friends for many years, and she was grateful that they were including her in their circle.

She and Lisa had clicked when they first met, and it was like they'd known each other forever. They were all about the same age, in their mid-fifties, and Marley felt that she had more of a community here on Nantucket than she'd ever had in California.

She'd been so busy raising her kids and growing what turned into a massively huge e-commerce business with her now ex-husband that she never had enough time to visit with friends. She'd thought Nantucket was just going to be a temporary stop and instead it turned into her forever home.

"Marley, how are things going with Mark? Paige asked.

Marley's second client, after Lisa, was Mark, a local photographer that was looking to see if he could sell some of his most admired prints online. She helped him set up a store and some marketing for it and in the weeks she spent consulting with him, they developed a friendship that recently had surprised both of them by turning into a romance. It was still very new, and Marley was cautious of getting too serious too soon. After the divorce, dating hadn't been on her radar at all. Until she met Mark.

"He's great. We're really enjoying each other's company. I did have a strange phone call though, right before I left to come over here." Marley had been so surprised by the call and debated whether to share with the girls, but decided she needed their input.

"So, out of the blue, Frank called me. I haven't talked to him in months. No reason to, now that the divorce is final. Apparently, he saw a picture of me and Mark online. Some of the photos from that charity gala we went to last week got picked up by the national news and someone brought it to his attention."

"That was a really good picture of you," Sue said.

"Thank you." Marley usually hated the way she looked in photos as she was always carrying an extra fifteen pounds or so, but she'd recently lost ten pounds and had been doing weight training so that she'd lost some inches and was down several sizes. She'd bought a new dress for the occasion, a rich royal blue, and it was very flattering.

Lisa's eyes narrowed. "Don't tell me he's jealous and wants you back?"

Marley laughed. "It's so ridiculous. But yes, he says that seeing my picture made him realize how much he misses me and that we never should have gotten divorced and he's an idiot and had a mid-life crisis."

"I agree with the idiot part," Lisa said dryly.

Sue lifted her wine glass and leaned forward. "Would you ever want to reconcile?"

Marley immediately made a face. "Absolutely not. I think he's lost his mind and just felt nostalgic and yes, probably a pang of jealousy when he saw me happy with someone else."

"A very handsome, nice someone else," Lisa added.

"So, you told him no, then?" Paige asked.

Marley nodded. "I did. I told him it was too late, and we'd both moved on and that I was happy. But he said he's coming to Nantucket next week and wants to meet for dinner, for old times' sake."

"You told him no, I hope?" Lisa said.

Marley hesitated. "I told him I'd think about it and he could call me when he got here. He's actually coming for some e-commerce conference at The Whitley. I'm going to it as well."

"You could just chat with him there, then?" Paige suggested.

"No. I told him I don't want to do that. If people see us there together, the media will be all over it. I don't want that. It might be easier to just see him briefly, have the conversation, and let him know it's totally not an option. I want to close that door firmly."

Sue topped off her wine glass and took a sip before

glancing at Marley. "You're curious to hear him out, see what he has to say. I would be too. Doesn't hurt to listen. And then tell him no with satisfaction."

Marley laughed. "That is sort of what I'm thinking. It is a nice boost for the ego. And I'm just glad that things are going well with Mark, so I'm not even remotely tempted."

Lisa lifted her glass. "Good! Let's drink to that."

CHAPTER 4

Taylor woke the next morning feeling like a new person. She'd gone to bed early, after a hot shower and a pizza delivered from one of the places Lisa had suggested. An hour or so of television and then she'd crashed hard. She eased out of bed and walked over to the window. It was a beautiful, sunny day, and she decided to venture out and take a walk on the beach before breakfast.

It wasn't as warm as it looked, though, and she was glad that she'd added an extra layer and a hat. She thought that she'd have the beach to herself since it wasn't quite seven, but there were already a few people out walking. She smiled as an excited golden retriever darted into the water and then quickly jumped out from the cold. It would be several months before it would be warm enough for swimming.

She walked down to the lighthouse and back, which took about an hour. A good walk. She'd worked up an appetite too—her stomach growled as she reached the dining room and smelled the hot food. Lisa was there already with her husband Rhett. She smiled when she saw Taylor.

"Good morning. Help yourself. There's a bacon and cheddar quiche today and some slow-cooker steel oats with peaches and brown sugar. I recommend a little of both if you can manage it. Please come join us."

Taylor helped herself to coffee, a sliver of the quiche, a few pieces of cantaloupe and a cup of the oatmeal, then brought everything over to the big round table where Lisa and Rhett were sitting.

"You remember my husband, Rhett?"

"Of course, how are you?"

Rhett nodded. "Nice to see you again."

They were joined a few minutes later by an older couple, Edith and Warren Douglas, who were there for their fortieth wedding anniversary.

"A trip to Nantucket has been on my bucket list and it's even lovelier than I'd imagined," Edith said. She explained that they'd just arrived two days ago and had been having a ball sight-seeing and shopping.

"We went to the Whaling Museum yesterday. That was really something," Warren said.

"What do you have planned for today?" Lisa asked.

Edith smiled. "This is our spoil ourselves day. We have massages booked downtown. We're going to catch a matinee and the popcorn will be our lunch. Because tonight we have reservations at The Whitley and are doing their tasting menu."

"Oh, that sounds wonderful," Taylor said. "I haven't eaten there, but it is supposed to be amazing."

Lisa smiled. "It is. Rhett and I went there a few months ago for my birthday and had the tasting menu. It's great for a special occasion. You'll love it."

"I can't wait," Edith said. She glanced at Rhett. "Lisa mentioned that you own a restaurant here too?"

"I do. Rhett's is right around the corner from here. It's not as fancy as The Whitley, but our food is good. It's typical New England, lots of fresh seafood, a few steaks and whatever else the chef feels like making."

Edith glanced at her husband. "Well, we'll have to make sure to go there one night, too."

"What are you up to today, Taylor? I think you mentioned you're seeing Abby and the girls tonight?" Lisa asked.

Taylor had chatted briefly with Abby the night before and was excited to see her and her sisters later that evening.

"Yes. I am going to head off and explore a bit and do a little shopping. I might pick up a dessert and some wine to bring to Abby's tonight, too."

"The supermarket here, Stop and Shop, has a pretty good bakery. And I'd stop by Bradford Liquors. The owner, Peter, is usually working, and he's great at helping with wine suggestions."

"Great, I'll be sure to stop by."

"Did Abby take you to Nantucket Threads when you visited?" Lisa asked.

"No, that doesn't sound familiar."

"It's a cute shop down by the wharf. The owner, Izzy, is a lovely girl. Her sister, Mia, stayed here for a few months when there was a fire at her condo. Marley, the woman that helped me with my online marketing, worked with Izzy too, to get an online store up for her shop. She has all kinds of gorgeous clothes and shoes."

Taylor grinned. "Sounds like that might need to be my first stop."

AFTER BREAKFAST, TAYLOR SHOWERED AND CHANGED, then headed downtown. Even though it was mid-morning on a Sunday, there were still a lot of people shopping and walking along Main Street. Taylor found a spot on a side street and set off to explore. When she reached Main Street and looked to her left, she saw Nantucket Threads a few doors down and made her way over to it. She stopped to check out the display window, which had several mannequins dressed in very cute outfits, pretty sweaters, floaty floral tops, dressy jeans and cowboy boots in a gorgeous caramel shade. An oatmeal-colored fisherman knit sweater caught her eye. It looked so New England and she didn't own anything like it.

She stepped inside and looked around the store. Lisa was right. It had many really cute things. She browsed for a bit, looking over some of the tops and the shoes, but found herself drawn to the sweater area and the fisherman knit style that she'd seen in the window. When

Taylor first walked in, a woman behind the counter smiled at her as she rang up a customer.

Taylor picked up one of the sweaters and held it up to her in the mirror to check the size.

"Those run true to size. You could probably do either a medium or a large depending how roomy you like it."

Taylor turned around, and it was the woman from the register. "If you'd like to try both sizes on, there's a fitting room in the back if you want to follow me."

"Thank you. Are you Izzy, by any chance? I'm staying at The Beach Plum Cove Inn and Lisa Hodges told me about your shop."

"Yes! That's me. That's so nice of Lisa."

Taylor grabbed two of the sweaters and followed Izzy to the fitting room.

"If you need an opinion, just holler," Izzy said.

Taylor tried the sweaters on and loved them both but went with the large as she did like them big and roomy. It was cold enough out that she could wear her new sweater to Abby's tonight.

As Izzy rang her up, she asked if Taylor was on vacation.

"No, I've actually just moved here. Lisa's daughter Abby was my college roommate and told me about a job here at the newspaper. I'm just staying at the inn until my rental is ready."

"Oh, welcome to Nantucket, then! I'm friends with Abby and her sisters, too. I'm sure I'll see you again, soon. Thanks for coming in."

"So where are you and your brother off to, tonight?" Abby asked her husband, Jeff. She'd just fed their daughter, Natalie, and settled her in her playpen, where Abby could keep an eye on her while she worked in the kitchen, getting dinner ready. The girls would be coming over in about an hour. Jeff had just come into the kitchen and was dressed and ready to go. He'd babysat the day before when Abby visited her mother and went shopping with her sister, and now it was his turn to head out. It was her suggestion, as she knew he had no interest in a girl's night.

"I think we'll just head to the Rose and Crown for a beer and a bite and maybe watch a game at the bar. We'll see."

She leaned over and gave him a quick kiss. "Have fun. I'll see you later."

As soon as Jeff left, she turned her attention back to the kitchen. Kate was bringing an appetizer, Kristen was making a salad and Taylor had said she'd pick up something for dessert, so Abby's focus was their main entrée. She was trying a new recipe that Jeff's mother had given her after Abby raved about it the last time they had dinner with his parents. It was a simple dish and Abby was hopeful that she wouldn't mess it up too badly. She knew the fish itself would be great. She got the striped bass from Trattel's Seafood, which Kate's husband Jack's family owned and operated.

The topping looked simple enough, just crushed

cracker crumbs mixed with a little beer, salt, pepper, and dill. Then the recipe said to spread a thin layer of mayonnaise on the fish and pat the stuffing on top, squeeze some lemon over it and bake until lightly browned.

It looked good when she slid it into the oven and she breathed a sigh of relief. It wasn't that Abby didn't like to cook, she just didn't have the same love for it that her sisters did. They could just throw things together and it would be amazing. She needed a clear recipe to follow.

She kept a close eye on the fish and when she took it out of the oven, she covered it with tin foil to keep it warm. It looked and smelled delicious. The girls would be arriving any minute, so she opened a bottle of chardonnay and poured herself a glass. She was excited to see her college roommate, Taylor, and thrilled that she'd actually taken a job on the island.

As much as she loved her sisters, Taylor was her best friend, and she hoped that the move would be a long-term one. She has a feeling it might be. Usually once people made the move to Nantucket, and fell in love with the lifestyle, they stayed.

Abby checked on Natalie, who was yawning already. She knew it wouldn't be long before she'd be out for the evening. Just as she was about to take her first sip of wine, there was a knock on the door and she heard laughter.

She opened the door and both of her sisters and Taylor stood on her doorstep.

"We all arrived at the same time," Kate said.

"Well, perfect then. Come on in. I just poured some wine."

They came in and Kate set her platter in the middle of the kitchen island and took off the foil covering.

"You made your bruschetta!" It was Abby's favorite appetizer. Thinly sliced toasted baguettes topped with Boursin cheese and a mix of diced tomatoes, garlic, olive oil and a drizzle of Balsamic vinegar.

"Peter said this would go well with the fish." Taylor handed her a bottle of Santa Margherita Pinot Grigio. "And I hope everyone likes brownies." She set a box of them on the kitchen counter.

"Thank you. The brownies look great. I've had this wine before and it's very good." She put it in the fridge to keep it chilled.

Kristen set her salad on the table and joined them at the island. Abby handed them each a glass of wine and they snacked on the bruschetta while they enjoyed their wine.

"Kate, I just saw the announcement online about your book being made into a TV series. Congrats, that's exciting," Taylor said.

"Thank you! I wasn't sure if we'd ever actually get it made. It was a brother-sister team that optioned it and it took forever before a studio actually gave it the green light. But Netflix is doing it as a ten-episode series, with the potential for a second season if it goes well," Kate said.

Abby was so proud of her sister. She'd moved home to Nantucket a few years ago after getting laid off from a Boston magazine and freelanced while writing her first mystery novel, which had always been a dream. She now had two books out and was working on a third.

Abby put the fish back in the oven for a few minutes to warm up, along with a casserole dish with mashed potatoes. Once everything was hot, they moved to the kitchen table and spent the next few hours eating and drinking and laughing. When they were totally full and nibbling on the brownies that Taylor brought, the conversation turned to Taylor's new job.

"So, Abby said you start at the paper tomorrow. Are you excited or nervous?" Kristen asked.

Taylor laughed. "Both. The job sounds perfect and I love that it's here on Nantucket." She glanced at Abby. "Your mother mentioned that you told her another girl just started too. I didn't realize they were hiring two people. Do you know her?"

"I know of her. Victoria is a local girl, a few years younger than us. I only just heard about this yesterday and mentioned it to my mother at breakfast. I heard she was working in Boston, but got engaged and moved home to Nantucket and in with her boyfriend. He does something here in real estate."

"What is she like?" Taylor looked a little nervous, and that was why Abby hadn't mentioned it. Victoria wasn't the warm, fuzzy type. She'd been head of the debate team and competitive in everything that she did—sports, and academics. Abby didn't think she and Taylor were likely to be close friends. But maybe she was wrong and Victoria had mellowed out since high school.

"She was a good student, captain of the field hockey team. I didn't really know her, though," Abby said.

Taylor took a bite of her brownie and looked thoughtful. "Well, business must be good if they hired both of us, right?"

"I'm sure it is." As far as Abby knew, the newspaper was doing well. And it probably was a good sign that they were able to hire two new people. Abby really didn't think it was anything to worry about.

"YOU DON'T LIKE YOUR STEAK?"

Marley snapped her attention back to the dinner she was sharing with Mark. It was Sunday night, and he'd called mid-day and invited her to his house for dinner. Usually, they either went out to one of the many great restaurants downtown, or Marley cooked in. She loved to cook and since he never let her pay when they went out, she enjoyed cooking for him. But now and then, he liked to have her over for dinner and cook on his grill. She glanced down at the perfectly cooked sirloin strip steak on her plate. She'd taken one bite, and it was delicious, but then her thoughts had drifted. Which was rude of her.

"I'm sorry. It's wonderful."

He looked at her closely. "Something on your mind? You looked a million miles away."

Marley sighed. She didn't want Mark to think there was anything to worry about with her ex. But she didn't want to not tell him and have him see a picture of the two of them at The Whitley event or elsewhere if she agreed to meet with him. She'd been thinking about the best way to do that and decided that going to any of the restaurants downtown was out of the question. They were both too high-profile, especially Frank, as he was still running the company that they'd built together.

The Attic was a public company, very well-known and one of the more volatile stocks due to the company's status as a front-runner in its e-commerce space. And unlike Marley, who had always hated media attention, Frank loved it. So, he wouldn't exactly mind if the media created a story if they saw the two of them together. In fact, the more she thought about it, if he wanted her back, he'd be all for it.

"Frank is in town for an e-commerce conference at The Whitley. He wants to meet for a drink."

Mark's eyes narrowed. "He wants you back?" He didn't seem at all surprised.

Marley nodded. "He says he does. I'm sure there's something driving this. His very young girlfriend probably dumped him."

"And he really thinks you might want to try again? Why would he think that?"

"Because he's a bit of a narcissist?" She smiled. "He's really not a bad guy. Our divorce wasn't because he cheated. We just grew apart. It was a mutual decision."

Mark took a sip of his scotch. There was a long moment of silence before he spoke again. "Have you ever thought about taking him back"

"Of course I have. The day I received the divorce

papers, I wondered if we were making a mistake. But the feeling passed quickly. We both wanted this and we've both moved on. At least I have."

"So why meet with him, then?"

"I think it might help give him closure—for it to sink in that it's really over. He might be sad now if a relationship ended, but running back to me isn't the answer."

Mark looked satisfied with that. "Good. I like what we've started, Marley. I'm not in any hurry to see it end."

She smiled. "I'm not either. I love spending time with you." Meeting Mark had taken Marley completely by surprise. He was just a year older than her and also divorced. When he'd been referred to her for help selling his photos online, she'd initially been intrigued by what he was looking to do. As she got to know him, she found they had a lot in common. He had a dry sense of humor that she appreciated and he was easy to be around.

At first, she'd thought it was just a nice new friendship, as the last thing on her radar was romance. But it snuck up on both of them and one night when they were watching live music at a bar by the beach, his hand had brushed against hers and her reaction had surprised her. He'd felt it too, and they'd had their first kiss that night. They'd been spending lots of time together ever since.

"So, he's just in town for a few days, for the conference, and then he'll be gone?"

"Yes, the conference ends on Thursday and he should fly back after that, I would think."

"Okay, enough about him. Save some room for

dessert. My mother dropped off one of her homemade apple pies today. Unless you're too full?"

She laughed. "There's always room for pie." She was glad she'd told him about Frank. She didn't want there to be any secrets between them.

CHAPTER 5

"Taylor, this is Victoria Carson. She's new here too, just started a week ago."

Blake was showing Taylor around the office, and they stopped in the newsroom first. The only other person there was a girl about Taylor's age. She was sitting at a desk and had a long blonde ponytail and a cellphone glued to her ear.

Victoria glanced her way and nodded. "Nice to meet you," she said quickly before turning her attention back to her phone. It looked like she'd been on hold and suddenly was chatting away, setting up a time to interview someone.

Blake chuckled as he continued leading Taylor around the office. "Victoria is a dynamo. I wish I had half her energy. She can be a little intense—don't let her intimidate you." He grinned, and Taylor wasn't sure if he was serious or joking.

So, she just smiled back and said nothing. He introduced her to a few others in the office. Mary, the front desk receptionist, was a warm and friendly woman in her sixties, Taylor guessed. Bill and Ernie, in the typesetting and graphic design area, looked to be in their early forties and both welcomed her. Their last stop was the ad sales department. Emily, Jason, and Franny were all on the phone and just waved hello as Blake and Taylor walked by.

"Franny's been here for as long as I can remember. All the clients love her. Jason and Emily have been with us for a few years and they're doing a great job, too. Revenues are up this year, which is why I was able to hire two full-time reporters. If we have more content for the paper, there will be more space for ads," he explained. Franny looked to be in her early fifties, and Emily and Jason looked close to Taylor's age, give or take a few years.

Blake continued talking as they reached his office.

"You both report to me. Along with Joe, our main reporter. He's been here for close to twenty years now. You'll meet him at some point. He's over at town hall right now. We use a few freelancers too on an as-needed basis. Let's head into my office now and discuss plan for the week."

They stepped into his office and Taylor stopped short, surprised to see a gorgeous golden retriever sleeping next to Blake's desk. The dog looked up and Blake introduced them.

"That's Richard. He's friendly. Did I mention on our Zoom call that this is a dog-friendly office? Richard comes to work with me most days and Ernie in graphics

...as Lady, his black lab here. You're welcome to ... your dog in too, if you like."

Taylor just nodded. She didn't have a dog yet. She didn't think it was fair to get one if she lived alone and was going to be at work all day. But—if she was allowed to bring the animal in—it was something to think about. She'd always loved having a dog.

An hour later, Taylor walked out of Blake's office with a stack of folders that he'd given her along with a printed sheet with local contact names and a calendar filled with due dates. She settled at her desk, which was next to Victoria's. Victoria jumped on a call as Taylor sat down and immediately turned her back to her, which was fine with Taylor. She had a busy week ahead of her and needed to get started.

Blake had explained that she and Victoria would each have assigned organizations they'd cover regularly and divvy up everything else that needed to be covered. They'd also have leeway to propose their own stories, and as long as Blake thought their ideas sounded good, they could run with them. He said Joe kind of did his own thing and didn't want to cover the stories they'd be working on. He mostly focused on town politics and police beats and various feature stories. Taylor was excited. This was so much better than obituaries and wedding announcements.

She was about to pick up the phone to call and schedule her first interview. Blake's first grade teacher had retired and opened a needlepoint shop on Main Street. So Taylor would meet with her and do a profile piece about her years of teaching on the island and her new chapter with the shop. It was a perfect first story for her and she looked forward to meeting Connie Day. Just as she was about to punch in the number, Victoria whirled around and fired questions at her.

"So sorry I couldn't talk earlier. Where are you from?"

"No problem. I just moved up here from Charleston."

"Were you working at a newspaper there?"

"Yes." Taylor didn't want to give the impression, though, that she had a lot of reporting experience. "It was a junior-level role. What about you?"

Victoria sat up a little taller in her chair. "I worked at the Boston Herald for three years as a reporter. It's a much faster pace in Boston. This is nice enough though."

"You're from Nantucket I hear," Taylor said.

Victoria looked surprised. "Did Blake mention that?"

"No. My friend Abby did. She said you went to school together. She's married now, but you might remember her as Abby Hodges."

Victoria thought for a moment and then nodded. "She was a few years ahead of me. How do you know her?"

"College roommates."

Victoria held up her hand to show off a huge diamond engagement ring. "This is why I came back. My boyfriend proposed. Both of our families are here and his job is too, so it made sense. It has been an adjustment though."

Taylor imagined after working at one of the two big papers in Boston, this might be very different.

Victoria stood and Taylor was surprised by how tall she was, easily five ten. "Okay, I'm out of here. Catch you later." She grabbed her purse and practically ran out the door.

Once she was gone, it was like all the energy had left the room. But Taylor didn't mind. It was easier to focus, and she wasn't as nervous to get on the phone and sound awkward since there was no one around to hear. She found the phone number Blake had provided and dialed his former teacher. She answered on the first ring.

"Mrs. Day? This is Taylor Abbott. Blake Ojala suggested I give you a call about a story for the paper…"

BLAKE FELT THE GENTLE NUDGE OF RICHARD'S NOSE against his leg—the dog's signal to be petted. He reached over and scratched behind his ears a few times until Richard flopped down and sunk his face between his front paws and fell fast asleep. He envied Richard's ability to do that, to shift gears so quickly and let everything go. Too often, Blake found himself unable to get to sleep, his thoughts racing.

He glanced out the open door of his office to where Taylor sat at her desk, a stack of folders in front of her. The newsroom was quiet, with both Joe and Victoria out of the office. He hoped that his gut instinct had been right and that Taylor would be a good addition to the office. She was such a newbie. All starry-eyed and earnest as she'd sat in his office. He had a good feeling about her, though. He liked that she was so excited about starting her new job and building a career in journalism. He'd been like that once, all enthusiasm and drive—feeling that anything was possible. And it had been. He'd done well.

His phone rang, and he sighed when he saw that it was his mother. He debated letting it go to voice mail, then felt guilty for wanting to evade her call. Better to get it over with. At least at work, he could keep it short.

"Hi, Mom."

"Hi, honey. What are you doing?"

Blake smiled. "I'm working, Mom. What are you up to?" He knew she was up to something. His mother rarely called just to chat. His parents spent the winter in Florida and his mother just arrived a week ago, almost a month ahead of his father, who was in no hurry to leave the warm weather.

"I'm on my way to the gym. Then Judy and I are having lunch at the Club Car. Judy mentioned yesterday that her daughter just got divorced, and we thought you two might want to meet up? Can I tell Judy you'll call her?"

Blake had a vague recollection of Judy's daughter as a spoiled, bossy blonde that spent a lot of time at the country club. She was friendly with his ex, Caroline. Very similar to Caroline, actually.

"No. I don't think so. Thanks anyway, Mom. I'm not big on setups."

His mother sighed. "Well, you're not going on any dates, are you? I just thought you two might hit it off."

"I can find my own dates."

"Hmm. Okay, well, if you change your mind, let us know. Bye honey."

Blake set the phone down and gazed out the window. It was less than six months since his last serious relationship ended. Dating wasn't high on his priorities at the moment. Much to his mother's dismay. His sister was married and his mother was anxious to see him settled, too. But the last thing he needed was to date someone who was so similar to his ex—and what he knew he didn't want. It was easier to not think about it, and to focus on work and enjoying Richard's company.

CHAPTER 6

Marley was annoyed with herself as she changed outfits three times before deciding on the one that flattered her the most. Why did she care that much about how she looked? It's not like she wanted Frank back. But she still wanted to look good. She knew her feelings for Frank were complicated. Even though she didn't want to get back together with him, they had been together for many years. She'd talked to her daughter the night before when she got home from dinner with Mark and learned, as suspected, that Frank had been dumped by the new girlfriend.

"Mom, he told us that he's going to win you back. He's not himself. I think this breakup really rattled him. I feel bad for him, but I still hope you won't take him back. You guys were so miserable at the end."

"Oh honey, I have no intention of getting back together with your father. I had a feeling it was something like that. I'll let him down easy."

"Thanks, and good luck, Mom. He sounds like he's on a mission."

Marley chuckled as she hung up the phone. She wasn't surprised by any of it. That was how Frank had always approached everything he did, full steam ahead and with total determination. It was an approach that usually worked well for him and for the company. But not this time. Still, she had once loved the man. It would be nice to see him.

She pulled her Audi sedan up to the entrance of The Whitley and handed the keys to the valet. The hotel looked beautiful, with lush landscaping out front and along the walkway and a breathtaking view of Nantucket Sound. It was an exceptional property, the nicest hotel on the island, by far. Marley had been there a few times, for drinks or for dinner. This would be the first time for a conference.

She made her way inside to the luxurious lobby, with its cool marble floors and vibrant flowers in crystal vases throughout the room. An easel with a poster pointed the way for the conference and she continued on down a long hallway to the main conference room where there was a registration desk by the door. She signed in, received a tote bag with an agenda and several free business books from people that were speaking at the event. There was also a name tag and lanyard, which she put around her neck and wandered into the ballroom to find a seat for the first lecture.

Frank was nowhere to be found. She guessed that he was still in his room, sleeping. They'd always been opposites about that. She was the early riser, and he stayed up until midnight most nights and rarely got up before nine. She found a seat near the front. The room filled up quickly and at eight o'clock sharp, the first presenter took the stage.

It was a busy morning and a fascinating one. Marley took lots of notes and her mind was whirling with new ideas to test and possibly suggest to her clients. There was still no sign of Frank at the mid-morning coffee break. It wasn't until they stopped again for lunch that she saw him. He'd already spotted her and was waving furiously from across the room.

She made her way over to him, and he pulled her in for a hug and a kiss on the cheek. His hair was still damp, which confirmed her theory that he'd slept in. But he looked good. She'd always found him attractive, though. He looked like he'd lost a few pounds. He still had a belly, but it was smaller than the last time she'd seen him. There was a bit more gray in his hair, but he hid it well with gel and he was newly shaved. He was making an effort.

"You look fantastic!" He exclaimed. His enthusiasm made her smile.

"Thanks, you look good too. Did you see any of the morning sessions?"

He grinned. "Nope, missed them all. I ran into some guys I knew when I checked in last night and we had dinner and drinks here at the hotel. Food was impressive. It ended up being a late night. A good time though."

"Figures you made it down just in time for lunch," Marley teased him.

He laughed. "You've got that right. Want to go find some seats?"

They made their way to the ballroom and found seats at one of the many round banquet tables. Marley was starving and looking forward to something good for lunch. They weren't disappointed. As soon as everyone was seated, waiters came around with bowls of clam chowder that were garnished with two fried clams. Marley enjoyed her soup while Frank held court at the table.

Several of the guys from the night before joined them and they quickly had a lively conversation going about the market and trends in retail shopping. Marley listened carefully and took it all in. She found it all fascinating and was enjoying the high energy level. That was one thing she missed working by herself. The energy at the company had been like that—continuous excitement as they all worked toward building something bigger and better.

They moved on to Caesar salad and then sautéed Nantucket scallops in a lemon butter sauce over whipped parsnips and broccolini. It was all delicious. Marley savored every bite while Frank inhaled his without missing a beat—he stayed engaged in intense discussion the whole time. He'd always been like that, usually the center of attention, and he loved being social. Marley enjoyed getting out too, but she was the quiet one in the relation-ship, which, for many years, had worked well for them.

She thought about what had happened with them and realized they'd drifted apart so slowly that neither was aware of it at first. Frank was just consumed with the business. It's all he thought about or talked about. And as much as she loved it too, after a while, it began to feel very unbalanced. She missed seeing their friends and spending time together as a couple. It was impossible to separate work from their personal relationship.

They'd tried counseling, but that hadn't worked. Frank never really saw that there was a problem, unfortunately, so he wasn't able to fix it. Eventually, Marley just grew tired of it and both of them were aware that things weren't right between them, and maybe they'd just come to the end of the relationship. At least, Marley had thought they were both on the same page about that.

When they were just about done eating, Frank turned his full attention her way. "This is such a great group of people. Are you having fun?"

Marley smiled. "So far, it's great. I learned a few things this morning that I want to try. And I knew the food would be good."

"I can't wait to catch up with you. What do you say about sneaking off for drinks at the bar, before dinner?" There were dinners and networking events both nights of the conference. Sitting alone with Frank at the bar didn't seem like a good idea to Marley. There were too many familiar faces here, and she didn't trust that a snapshot of them wouldn't wind up on social media and the speculation would begin.

"You won't want to miss the pre-dinner drinks with everyone. This is a great group for networking. Plus, I don't want anyone to get the wrong idea if they see us having drinks by ourselves."

Frank grinned. "Well, I wouldn't mind that. But you're right about the networking. I probably shouldn't miss that. How about dinner on Thursday night then? I fly out first thing Friday morning. We can go anywhere you want."

"How about takeout at my house? There is a lot of media on the island right now and I don't want to risk being seen out anywhere. Plus, you haven't seen my house yet."

He nodded. "Okay, just text me the address and I'll find it. You'll be here tonight too for the dinner and evening events?"

"Yes, I'll be here. The networking is good for me too." She hoped to pick up a new client or two, possibly.

He looked surprised for a moment and then smiled. "Yes, I suppose it might be. How is the consulting going?" She knew he hadn't given it a thought until she brought it up, which was typical.

"It's going very well. I'm really enjoying it."

"Good, and that's the kind of thing you can do from anywhere, right?"

She knew where he was going with that. "Yes, pretty much. I'm thrilled that I can live here on Nantucket and still do work that I enjoy."

CHAPTER 7

"Do you think this needs anything else?" Lisa handed a spoonful of tomato sauce to her daughter Kate, who was sitting at the kitchen island. It was Wednesday night and Lisa had invited Kate and Kristen over for dinner when Kate mentioned earlier that her husband, Jack, was out of town for the night with his brother. She'd checked with Abby and Chase too, but they weren't able to make it. Lisa handed a spoon with sauce to Kristen, too.

"It's delicious. Maybe a hint more salt?" Kate said.

"I think it's perfect," Kristen said.

Lisa added a few shakes of salt to the pot and gave the sauce a final stir. "Meatballs are in the oven and need about ten more minutes. We can have some wine while we wait." She poured glasses of cabernet for the three of them and set a box of crackers and a block of cheddar cheese on a plate and brought it to the island.

"Is Rhett going to be home for dinner?" Kate asked.

Lisa shook her head. "No, he's working tonight. He won't be home until later." She settled into a chair and carved off a slice of cheese.

"How's business at the restaurant?" Kristen asked as she reached for her wineglass.

"Busy. Which is good." Lisa frowned, though, thinking about what Rhett had said. "Rhett suspects that someone at the restaurant might be skimming some money somehow. He said his numbers seem short lately on some nights."

"Everything is computerized though, isn't it?" Kate asked. "How could someone do that?"

"He's not sure. He's not even positive that it's happening, just that the numbers seem low, based on the amount of food they are going through. There's a disconnect somewhere."

"That's unsettling," Kristen said.

"It really is. He's not happy to think that someone that works for him could be stealing. I know it happens though." Lisa knew it was stressing Rhett out and she felt for him. She decided to change the subject.

"How's the new book coming along, honey?" She asked Kate.

Kate made a face as she reached for her wine. "Slowly. So slowly. The past few days have been like pulling teeth. It's always like that for me at the beginning of a new book though. I don't really know the story yet."

"Have you ever tried outlining? That seems like it might be less stressful," Lisa suggested.

"You would think so, but I've learned that I'm just not

an outliner. I tried it once and then felt like I'd already written the book."

Kristen smiled. "Tyler said the same thing. He doesn't outline either. You just have to trust the creative process."

Kate nodded. "It's similar to your painting, isn't it? You kind of feel your way through it?"

"Yes, that's it exactly. I never know where I'm going with a painting until my brush touches the canvas."

"I don't know how the two of you do it. I'm so proud of both of you." Lisa stood. "I think those meatballs must be about ready and then we can eat."

She added the meatballs to the pot of sauce and piled cooked pasta in three bowls and added a generous helping of meatballs and sauce to each. They ate at the kitchen table where Kate could still have a good view of the twins, Toby and Annabella, who were sound asleep in their playpen. They'd fallen asleep on the drive over, stirred for a moment and fell right back asleep. Lisa suspected they'd be wide awake soon enough, though.

"What's new with you and Tyler?" Lisa asked Kristen as they dug in.

"He's heads down, finishing up a book. I don't see much of him when he's at this stage. He works all day and night in a mad rush to get it all down. But, he thinks he'll be done with his first draft by tomorrow and he wants to go to Boston for the weekend to celebrate."

"How fun," Kate said. "Do you know where you'll stay?"

"He said something about an Airbnb on Charles Street."

"Oh, that's a great spot. You'll be able to walk every-where and there are so many romantic restaurants right there." Kate sounded excited for her sister.

"That sounds like a wonderful weekend. It's been a long time since you did something like that," Lisa said.

"I know. Ages. We're both looking forward to it," Kristen said. Lisa thought back and realized the last time Kristen had gone off-island was when Tyler went to a rehab on the Cape. He'd gone through a rough time after his mother died and relapsed with alcohol briefly. But he seemed to be doing well now.

Lisa had been concerned about the relationship initially as Kristen had been dating someone before that who was separated and she eventually realized he was in no hurry to finalize the divorce. Lisa just wanted to see her happy, and it seemed like she'd found that with Tyler.

Lisa smiled. "Well, take lots of pictures. I can't wait to hear all about it when you come home."

"How was your first day?" Lisa asked over breakfast the next morning. Taylor had just loaded her plate with cheesy scrambled eggs, crispy bacon, and sour-dough toast. She figured she'd have a hearty breakfast since it was available and eat light for lunch. It was early, just a few minutes past eight, and they had the room to themselves.

"It was good. Busy. I spent most of my time getting familiar with the office and computer system and setting up some interviews for the rest of the week. I have my first one this morning as soon as I leave here."

"How exciting. Who are you interviewing?"

"Connie Day. She just opened a new needlepoint shop downtown and retired from teaching. My boss, Blake, was in her class years ago."

Lisa nodded. "I remember Connie. The girls all had her. Chase is the only one that had a different teacher. They loved her. I didn't realize she'd opened a needle-point shop. I'll have to go check that out. I haven't done needlepoint in years."

"Where's Rhett today?" This was the first time he hadn't been with Lisa at breakfast since Taylor arrived.

"He went into work early today to do some ordering. Which means he'll be home early tonight. I think we may go out for a change. I have a hankering for the fish tacos at Millie's. Has Abby taken you there yet?"

Taylor smiled. "Yes. Last time I was here. We split a few things. I loved the scallop and bacon tacos. And the margaritas, of course."

"Of course. I haven't tried those tacos. Kate mentioned them, too. I always seem to order the same thing. One of these days maybe I'll try something different."

TAYLOR ARRIVED AT CONNIE'S SHOP FIVE MINUTES BEFORE nine and parked a few doors down. At nine sharp, she knocked on the front door and a moment later it was opened by a petite woman with short, curly gray hair and a big smile.

"You must be Taylor! Come in." She held the door open wide and Taylor stepped inside.

"Thank you for meeting with me," Taylor said. She looked around the shop. It was adorable. Small but decorated in soft blue, gray and creamy white. Soothing seascape paintings hung on the wall and were all for sale.

Connie noticed her gaze and smiled. "Those are all done by local artists. We have a lot of talent on this island. They are all different areas of Nantucket."

"They're beautiful." Also hanging on the wall were many finished needlepoint projects, nicely framed and situated by all the materials a crafter would need to do it themselves.

"Did you make all the needlepoints?" There were at least two dozen of them throughout the room.

Connie's eyes twinkled. "I did. Needlepoint has always been my passion. I miss teaching, of course, but I'm also looking forward to this next chapter of my life."

Taylor noticed a large calendar near the register that was also a whiteboard, and in bright purple marker, various classes were listed each week.

"You're doing classes too?"

Connie nodded. "Yes, I thought that might be fun. I'm doing all levels, beginning to advanced, so there's something for everyone. And then of course they'll want to keep going and buy more materials!"

Taylor smiled. "My grandmother used to do a lot of needlepoint. She loved it."

"It's a wonderful creative outlet. Did your mother do it too?"

Taylor tried not to laugh at the thought. "No. My mother wasn't the needlepoint type. She could never sit still that long."

"It might be good for her. It's very calming. But, of course, it's not for everyone."

Connie walked her around the shop and showed Taylor everything. Connie was especially excited about her Christmas section. "I know it's not the season now, but lots of needlepointers work on holiday projects year-round. Ornaments are especially popular." A two foot tall artificial tree stood in the corner, covered in assorted needlepoint ornaments that looked both festive and homey at the same time.

"Those are cute. They don't look too hard to do either. Are they good for beginners?"

"They're not hard at all. If you're interested, dear, you should think about coming to my beginners' class. It covers the basics and everyone will make several ornaments. It's once a week for two months, starting next Tuesday."

"Maybe I will." There wasn't a whole lot to do on Nantucket mid-week in March, and it sounded kind of fun to Taylor. "Maybe I'll see if my friend Abby is interested and wants to come with me."

"Is she a local girl?"

"Yes, her maiden name is Hodges. She has two sisters too, Kate and Kristen."

"Of course! Lovely girls. Please tell Abby I said hello.

Now, let's go into the sitting room and have some tea and we can chat some more. This is also where the classes will be held."

Taylor followed her into an adjoining room that had a big round table in the middle and a tiny kitchen area with a small refrigerator, coffee maker, and an electric tea kettle. Connie quickly heated up some water and poured two cups of herbal tea. The flavor was vanilla caramel, and it smelled heavenly. She also set out a delicate china plate with buttery shortbread cookies.

"Please have a cookie, or two. They go so well with this tea."

Taylor really wasn't hungry after that big breakfast, but she still reached for a cookie anyway and nibbled on it as Connie told her all about her days as a teacher. It was clear she had loved the job. She was equally passionate about needlepoint though, and Taylor had a feeling she was going to enjoy her new venture.

"So, it's perfect. I'll be able to sit out front and do my needlepoint in between chatting with customers and ringing them up. I'll be getting paid to do what I love."

"It sounds like it will be fun for you," Taylor agreed.

Connie looked reflective. "You know, my grandfather told me when I was about to graduate high school that if I could find a way to make money doing something I love, that it wouldn't feel like work. I think that is very true as I really did love teaching. And now this is just for fun, so if I make a little money at it too, well, that will just be gravy."

Taylor thought about that. She hadn't yet had the

experience of loving her job, but was hopeful that maybe she'd found what she was supposed to do.

"I've heard that before, too. My mother and stepfather are both realtors and they live and breathe real estate. They truly love it."

"And I bet they do well at it?"

"They do."

"So let's talk about you now. You're new at the paper?"

"Yes, I just started yesterday. You're my first interview," Taylor admitted.

"Well, I'm honored. You're working for good people. Blake and his father have done a nice job with that paper. Blake told me that his father is semi-retired now and Blake is running the show."

"That's right. I report to him."

"He's a good boy, Blake is. Well, of course he's not a boy anymore. But I think of all my former students that way. He was a very good student. Always had a lot of questions. So, it looks like he found the right career for himself. He needs to settle down, though, and find a nice girl. I imagine he's a little gun shy still though." Connie paused dramatically, and Taylor had no idea what she was referring to. So she said nothing and waited for Connie to continue. She didn't have to wait long.

"He was engaged for several years and was supposed to get married the weekend of Nantucket Stroll this past December. I'd been invited to the wedding and was looking forward to it. Though I didn't know Caroline, his fiancée. She wasn't local. Pretty girl, but I heard that she was from Boston and dumped him a month before the wedding. I don't know the whole story. Maybe they'd been having problems. I suppose that's better than a month after the wedding though, right?"

"Yes, as awful as that sounds, I'd rather have it happen before than after."

"It was going to be quite the wedding, too. The reception was going to be at The Whitley. That's the best hotel on Nantucket, and the most expensive too. At least Blake didn't have to worry about that."

"No?" Taylor tried to keep up.

"Caroline was from a very wealthy old Boston family and of course they were paying for the reception." She paused for a moment before adding, "Blake will be quite the catch for someone. He's smart and if you've noticed, he's not hard on the eyes either." Connie grinned.

Taylor had the feeling that Connie might be trying to play matchmaker.

"Blake is very handsome," she agreed. "I might be tempted if he wasn't my boss. I'm sure that wouldn't be allowed."

Connie frowned. "Well, I don't know why not. That seems silly to me. We have to grab love wherever we find it."

Taylor smiled as she looked down at her notes. "Is there anything else you can think of that we haven't covered? Anything you'd like people to know?"

"Well, just tell them if they want to stop by and say hello, I'm here every day, except Sunday, from ten to six."

CHAPTER 8

W hen Taylor arrived at the newsroom and settled at her desk to start working on Connie's story, Victoria ended her call and stood. Taylor noticed she was a bit more dressed up than she had been the day before. Her hair was down and slightly curled into long, loose waves, and she had more makeup on too.

"Well, I'm off, see you later."

"Who are you interviewing?" Taylor asked.

Victoria grinned. "Whoever will agree to talk to me. There's a big e-commerce conference at The Whitley and I have a press pass. I'm going to spend the rest of the day there. There are a lot of famous tech people attending, so there might be a hot story or two."

That didn't sound interesting to Taylor at all. Especially to go by herself to a conference where she knew no one. But Victoria seemed excited about it.

"Good luck! Hope you have fun."

"Thanks! I intend to." She grabbed her purse and iPad and left.

Taylor turned her attention back to her notepad and opened up a Word doc on her computer and spent the rest of the morning turning her notes into a story. She was just about done and lost in her work when she heard footsteps and looked up. Blake walked by holding a paper cup of coffee and a stack of mail. He stopped when he reached her desk.

"How'd the meeting with Connie go?"

"Good. She's a sweetheart and her shop is really cute. She said you were one of her favorites."

He smiled. "I bet she says that about all her students."

Taylor laughed. "She might actually. She really loved that job."

"I hope she's not too sad about retiring?"

"Not at all. She spoke fondly about her years of teaching, but she seems excited about the shop. She wants me to take one of her needlepoint classes."

He chuckled. "Are you into arts and crafts?"

"Well, no. But it did sort of look like fun. I'm just about to email you my story. I hope it turned out okay."

"You should take the class. And go ahead and send the story. I'll take a look. Do you have any lunch plans?" It was almost noon and Taylor hadn't even thought about lunch yet.

"No plans. I figured I'd run out and grab a sandwich at some point."

"If you can wait until one, we can go to lunch. I'll read this over and we can discuss it then."

"Oh, ok. Sure." Taylor didn't expect to get feedback that quickly or to have lunch with her boss.

"How do you feel about barbecue? I thought we'd head over to B-Ack Yard BBQ? It's close by and always good."

"Love it. I haven't been there yet."

By one, Taylor was good and hungry. It was an easy walk from the offices on India Street to the barbecue place which was right on Straight Wharf by the ferries. The restaurant was busy when they arrived, but the host recognized Blake and quickly found a table for them.

The smell was intoxicating. Taylor had thought she'd order a salad, but once she stepped inside, the scent of the grill and smoked meats tempted her. She followed Blake's lead and ordered a chopped smoked brisket sandwich with coleslaw and potato salad. While they waited for their meals, Blake handed her a printout of her story. It was marked up with lots of red and he explained where he'd like to see changes.

"Overall, you did a very good job. These are just style things to be aware of so we have consistency in how we deliver the news."

Taylor listened and took it all in, but was a little concerned by what looked like a sea of red marks. She worried that it wasn't good enough.

Blake seemed to read her mind. "Seriously, it's fine.

Don't worry. This is a learning process. We all went through it."

Taylor relaxed a little at that. "I'll work on the changes when we get back."

"If you can get it to me by mid-day tomorrow, we can run it this week. It's a good story, Taylor. I thought that would be a nice first assignment for you."

She smiled. "It really was fun. I enjoyed talking to Connie. She was a big fan of yours, too."

"Yeah? What did she say?"

"Well, that you were a great student, like I mentioned before. But, she also said she had been looking forward to your wedding." She paused and then gently added, "She said it was going to be over the Stroll weekend."

He sighed. "Yeah. She was on the guest list. Did she say anything else about it?"

"Only that she didn't know what happened but was glad that you wouldn't get stuck paying for it because it was going to be an expensive one."

Blake laughed. "She's right about that. It was going to be one of those ridiculous over-the-top weddings. I'd suggested having this place cater for a barbecue on the beach this summer, but Caroline hated that idea. Really, what it came down to was we wanted different things, and not just when it came to the wedding. We dated for a long time, were engaged for over three years, which I guess should have been a sign."

Blake didn't seem all that upset about the breakup. That seemed like a good thing.

"The final clincher was that Caroline wanted us to

move off-island and to live in Dover, a suburb of Boston. She actually thought I could do that and still run the paper. I never even told her I'd consider it, but I think she assumed because she stated it that it would happen. When she finally realized I was serious about not leaving the island, she ended things."

"I don't see how you could have done that, either. What made her think it was possible?"

"She expected me to commute, spending three or four days a week here. We own the building, and I live right above it, so I suppose that would be doable. But I didn't want to do it. When I get married, I don't want a part-time marriage, which is what that would be."

Their waiter arrived with their sandwiches and they both dug in and were quiet for a few moments before Blake spoke again.

"So, what do you think about the barbecue?"

Taylor thought she was going to need a long walk on the beach when she got home from work because she was eating every last bite of her sandwich.

"It's amazing. And a little dangerous that it's so close to the office."

Blake laughed. "It is. But, I almost never take a full lunch hour. I usually eat at my desk. But, you are certainly welcome to go to lunch every day if you like."

Taylor smiled. "I'd love to, but I couldn't eat like this every day."

"It's a great after work spot for drinks too. We all do that now and then. So, you know all about me. Tell me more about you. What brought you to Nantucket?"

"Well, as you know, I started out in advertising and it was a good opportunity. I learned that I want a career in journalism. But I wanted to do more and ideally work at a paper. My mother was pushing me to be a proper Southern girl, join the Junior League and find a husband and ideally get a job in real estate like her. But, I'm not my mother."

"I don't see you in real estate," Blake agreed.

Taylor laughed. "Not at all. That was the only thing my mother liked about me moving to Nantucket. It's apparently a great market for real estate sales and she encouraged me to join a local office here."

"Well, she is right about that. There's a lot of money on Nantucket. The homes are wildly expensive." He took his last bite of his sandwich and grinned. "So, I take it there are no serious husband candidates either?"

"No. I'm very single. Finding a husband is the last thing on my mind. Nantucket seems more laid back than Charleston when it comes to that. It's one of the things I really liked about it when I visited Abby, my college room-mate, a few times."

"That's right, you're good friends with Abby and her husband, Jeff. I play hockey in a men's league with him in the winter."

"When she told me about the opening at the paper, it seemed almost too good to be true. I applied immediately, but I was worried that I didn't have enough actual reporting experience. So, I'm really grateful for the opportunity."

He smiled. "Well, compared to Victoria, you don't

have as much experience, no. But that's okay. I needed to hire for two roles and it made sense to me to hire two people with different levels of experience. You can learn from her and from Joe. And because you are more junior, you'll handle some of the assignments that neither of them will want to do," he admitted.

She laughed at that. "I'll handle whatever you need. It's all new to me, well, other than obituaries and birth announcements." She hoped that those wouldn't come her way though.

"I like your attitude. And don't worry, you won't get stuck doing those. We have a part-timer that works one day a week for a few hours. Nantucket is a much smaller place and we don't have the volume that a big city would."

Taylor smiled. "Well, I'll admit that I'm happy to hear that. But, if you ever got stuck, I could do it."

"I appreciate that." Blake put down the company credit card when the waiter brought the bill.

"Thank you for lunch. This was really wonderful."

CHAPTER 9

Marley went home, walked along the beach in front of her house for about a half hour, then took a long soak in her oversized tub. She stayed there until the water grew cold, then reluctantly got out, dried off and dressed in her favorite old jeans and soft sweatshirt that she'd bought her first week on Nantucket at her client, Izzy's shop. It was such a touristy sweatshirt with big letters that said Nantucket on it and was a unique pinkish red shade known as Nantucket Red. She'd loved it at first sight.

She settled in her kitchen with her laptop and did a little work, checking emails mostly, before it was time to call the order in. She did know what Frank's favorites were, so she ordered a bunch of things they both liked.

He arrived a few minutes early, which was the norm for him. She opened the door and he handed her a big paper bag of food.

"It was ready when I got there and there's no traffic on Nantucket. Took no time to get here."

"Thanks. Let's go in the kitchen." She set the bag on the island and was about to put all the containers out so they could help themselves.

"Can you give me a tour first? I'd love to see the rest of your place."

"Sure." Marley walked him around her house, which she had loved at first sight. It was right on the ocean and was relatively small in comparison to all the McMansions on the island. It had three bedrooms, a small office, a cozy family room, lots of floor-to-ceiling windows with incredible ocean views and an oversized farmer's porch that wrapped around the whole house.

"This is really something," Frank said as she led him into her office. It wasn't very big, but the view was amazing. "How do you get any work done? I'd be distracted by that view."

Marley smiled. "You get used to it. I find it really relaxing."

They made their way back to the kitchen, and she set about opening the various containers and getting some plates and utensils out.

"Start helping yourself. What would you like to drink? I have beer and wine."

"No scotch?"

"Beer and wine," she repeated.

"I'll take a beer then."

She got it for him, poured herself a glass of chardonnay and joined him at the island. They chatted easily as they ate, mostly comparing notes about the conference. Once they finished eating though and Marley put all the food away, Frank got more serious.

"I really do want to try again and make this work with you. We were so good, for so long. Don't you want to see if we can get the magic back?" He looked so sincere that for two seconds Marley actually wavered before realizing it was just his usual charm. It wasn't real.

"Frank. What's really going on with you? Nothing has really changed with us. We fell out of love a long time ago."

He sighed. "I was afraid you'd say that. You're sure? We have so much in common. You could come back to San Francisco, join the company again."

She shook her head sadly. "Thank you, but no. I don't want to do any of that. Nantucket is my home now, and I like what I'm doing. I loved working with you and helping to build the business, but I've really moved on." She reached out and put her hand on his arm. "What's really going on?"

He was quiet for a long moment. "Tina left me for a twenty-five-year-old guitar player that makes tens of millions in some band. I can't compete with that. I feel old."

Marley bit her tongue. Agreeing that he was old wasn't going to help the situation. She chose her words carefully.

"I'm sorry that didn't work out for you. I'm sure it was fun for a while. Have you considered looking for someone closer to your own age? With more common interests?"

He took a sip of his beer. "Well, yes. That's why I'm here."

"And you don't want to be alone." She suspected that was really at the heart of it.

"Who does?"

"I thought I did, actually. I enjoyed being by myself for a while, when I first arrived here. I explored the island, met some people, and relaxed. And then when I least expected it, I met Mark."

"Is it serious with the two of you?"

She smiled. "Neither of us is dating anyone else. And we enjoy each other's company. We were friends first."

He nodded. "I'm not sure I know how to do that."

"You'll figure it out. Just live your life. Take it one day at a time and see where it leads you."

They chatted a bit longer before Marley walked him to the door. It was early, but they were both yawning and he had an early flight the next day.

She gave him a hug goodbye. "It was really good to see you."

He hugged her back and kissed her cheek. "You too." He grinned. "If you change your mind... you know how to reach me."

———

"YOU HEADING OUT SOON? EVERYTHING IS DONE, AND it's getting late. It was a good night again." Rhett looked up at the sound of Nora's voice, his main manager at the restaurant. She'd been with him since the beginning, and he trusted her implicitly. But he hadn't mentioned his suspicions to her about the stealing yet. He wanted to, but he'd talked to Lisa about it and she'd advised him to keep quiet and try to figure it out himself first. He didn't think for a minute that Nora was involved, but Lisa had a good point, because he couldn't imagine any of his employees stealing from him.

It had happened before, though. At his New Jersey restaurant years ago, before they put in computer systems, there was a waitress that everyone loved, Lorraine. She was older and had a gift for baking. She made birthday cakes for everyone and they were amazing. So everyone loved her. And no one suspected that she was the one that had an elaborate system for skimming off the top.

They knew something was going on but never looked closely at Lorraine until she got herself in trouble one night when he happened to overhear her bragging about how well she'd done with her tips. That was Lorraine's one flaw. She was a bit of a one-upper and always seemed to make more than everyone else. But the night Rhett happened to overhear the amount she said she made, alarm bells went off. Because her numbers didn't add up. The restaurant hadn't been that busy that night. There was really no way she could have made the amount she claimed.

So he took a closer look at her orders that night and sure enough, they didn't add up to an amount that would generate the tip number she'd boasted about. But that wasn't enough to prove it was her. He needed to figure out what she was doing and catch her in action. He also noticed that all of her checks that night were credit cards. That wasn't totally unusual, but it made him think of what she could be doing, and he had a theory.

He talked to Randy, the head chef, and swore him to secrecy because they didn't know anything for sure yet. But Randy also agreed to pay close attention to Lorraine's orders the next time she worked, and to keep count of her meals' total. He also agreed to keep an eye on the order stack and see if Lorraine removed any orders from the spindle at any point.

It only took one night. Once again, at the end of the evening, all of Lorraine's cashed out checks were credit card sales and the tip amount she boasted about earning was simply too high. She was a good waitress and customers loved her, but Rhett knew they didn't all overtip all the time. While Lorraine was doing her closing sidework, Rhett went into the kitchen and checked with Randy.

"She removed two orders from the spindle. A two-top and a four-top. I could see one mistake, but not two," Randy said. "And we made all six of those meals. She pulled them hours later, after they cashed out. If you look though you can see all of her order slips have the outside corner folded in. That made it easy for her to quickly find the right one."

Rhett had been both impressed at her cleverness and bitterly disappointed to discover that one of his favorite employees was regularly ripping him off. And she'd worked for him for over ten years! He never in a million years would have suspected Lorraine. And it was for that reason that he couldn't share his suspicions with Nora. He sighed. He wished that he could, as maybe she could help him figure this out.

Instead, he smiled. "I'm heading out shortly. Have a good night, Nora, and thanks for everything."

Rhett stayed for another half hour, looking at the evening's totals and trying to find something that jumped out to explain what was going. But he couldn't find anything. On paper, it all looked fine, but for the volume of business they were doing, the numbers still felt slightly off to him. He looked over all the numbers again until his eyes felt tired and he decided to call it a night. He'd sleep on it and see if any new ideas came to him.

THE NEXT MORNING, AT BREAKFAST, RHETT WAS surprised to see Marley sitting with Lisa in the dining room when he meandered in, later than usual. Lisa had already gone to bed by the time he got home the night before. He'd texted her and told her not to wait up. No sense in both of them losing sleep. So, he ended up sleeping in later than usual and it was almost nine by the time he poured his first cup of black coffee and joined Lisa and Marley.

"I invited Marley to come by for breakfast," Lisa explained. "We're going to go for a walk after we eat."

"Nice to see you again." Rhett considered Marley a friend too as she'd stayed at the inn for several months when she first came to Nantucket. "How's business?"

"I was just telling Lisa that it's really going well. I picked up a few new clients at an industry conference this week at The Whitley."

"That's great."

"I told Marley what's going on at the restaurant. Did you have any luck last night figuring things out?" Lisa asked.

Rhett shook his head. "No. I went over the numbers every which way and nothing looks out of place, but it still feels off to me. And I checked the inventory and we're already lower than we should be on a few items."

"You think someone is skimming somehow off the top?" Marley said.

He nodded. "My gut says yes. But I have no idea who it could be."

"We had this happen with our business a few times over the years. And it's never who you'd expect. People steal for all kinds of reasons. Some because they're desperate and need the money and others for the thrill of it."

"How did you catch them?" Lisa asked.

Marley smiled. "We finally hired a security company, and they installed hidden cameras inside the warehouse and at the entrances. That's what you may want to do, Rhett. It's not expensive, and it's a good safety thing to have anyway, especially the outdoor cameras. They link up to your computer or phone, and whenever there's movement, they film. So, if anyone ever breaks in for instance, you'll have it for the police."

Rhett found the suggestion intriguing. "I don't like the

idea of hidden cameras inside the restaurant all the time, but maybe for a week or so until we figure out what is going on and then after that, after we close for the night. And I really like the idea of permanent ones by the back door. If someone is taking inventory out of the building we'll see it. Thanks for the suggestion." Rhett finally felt hopeful that this could be a solution to find out what was really going on.

"You also might start paying closer attention to what everyone is doing during the shift. More than you do now," Marley said. "We sort of had our blinders on because we weren't looking for anything shady to happen, but when we started really paying attention, we also noticed little things we'd missed that were happening right under our noses."

"You can do that Rhett. You're always floating around, helping out everywhere anyway," Lisa said.

"That's true. And you're right, Marley. If I'm not looking for something, I'm likely to miss it. I will make an effort to be more aware. And I'm going to call someone today to see about getting those cameras installed."

"I used someone for my house, am happy to pass on their info. I got used to having the security cameras in San Francisco and once I moved into my own place, as safe as Nantucket is, I still like the security of having them."

"Thanks, I'd appreciate that."

THE NEXT MORNING, AT EIGHT-THIRTY, RHETT MET ALAN, the alarm guy that Marley referred to him at the restaurant. He was grateful that Alan had a cancellation and was available to get it done that quickly. First thing in the morning before anyone else arrived was perfect timing, too.

It took maybe forty-five minutes for Alan to hook everything up. He put small cameras above the front and back doors. They were so small that they were easy to miss and Rhett hoped no one would look up and notice them. For the ones inside, he cleverly hid them so that they wouldn't be obvious. One pointed at the register out front where people cashed out and the other was hidden at the bar and would monitor the register there.

Once everything was hooked up, Alan showed him how to look on his phone or iPad to see what the camera recorded. He could see the filming live as it happened and it would all be saved to view anytime.

"If you have any questions, let me know. You're all set now. I hope it helps you find out what is happening," Alan said.

Rhett hoped so, too. Because if this didn't work, he was out of ideas.

CHAPTER 10

Taylor's first week flew by. She was so busy and was enjoying all of it. She met Joe, the senior reporter, on her second day. He was older, in his early forties, and kept to himself. He popped in and out of the office and spent a lot of time down at town hall and the police and fire departments. He was very focused and his stories were more serious in-depth features or local updates on politics or crime. Taylor sensed that he didn't have much interest in chatting with her or Victoria.

She couldn't quite figure Victoria out either. One minute, she seemed semi-friendly when she was bragging about her real estate boyfriend or an obviously expensive purse that Taylor had admired. Other times, she barely said two words to her. Though Taylor told herself that maybe she was just really focused on her work.

Mid-day on Friday, Blake strolled through the office

and stopped at their desks. "How'd it go at the conference, Victoria? Anything interesting there?"

"Yes! I got a few hot stories actually and some great pictures. I just emailed them to you. There were some really well-known people there and I bet one of my stories might even go viral." She grinned and looked pleased with herself.

Blake raised an eyebrow. "No kidding, viral? I'll take a look at that. Any celebrity sightings? I heard that Cami Carmichael is filming something here, might be something interesting there."

"No, I didn't see any celebrities like that. Just big tech types. I'll keep an eye out for that, though. I'd love to do a real celebrity story."

"Cami Carmichael is on the island?" Taylor was a huge fan and had seen all of her romantic comedies.

"She's staying out by The Whitley Hotel, and dates the chef. That's all I know," Blake said. "Though if they are filming a movie, there could be some other famous stars around too. Keep your eyes out."

Victoria grinned. "If they are here, I will find them!"

"Great. The other thing I wanted to mention is we're shutting down at four today. After-work drinks at the B-Ack Yard BBQ. First round is on me. Hope you both can make it."

"I wouldn't miss it!" Victoria said.

"I'll be there too." Taylor looked forward to having her first after-work drinks with her new co-workers.

At four o'clock sharp, Mary put the reception desk answering machine on, and they all headed out. Taylor chatted with Mary as they walked the short distance to the restaurant.

"Does this happen often?" Taylor asked her.

"At least once or twice a month since Blake took over. It's really a great place to work. How are you liking it so far?"

"I'm really liking it. A lot." Taylor felt like she might have finally found a job she could love and stay with for a long time. For the first time, she found herself excited to go to work each morning, and the days flew by.

Taylor noticed the odd spelling of the restaurant's name and asked Mary is there was a reason for it.

She laughed. "Yes, ACK is a nickname for Nantucket, and the official airport letters."

"Oh, okay now it makes sense."

Even Joe joined them, along with everyone in sales and the two guys in the graphics department. They took over half the bar, and it was a lively group. Taylor found that outside of the office, with a beer in his hand, Joe actually had a conversation with them. And he was interesting to talk to.

"I have an interview at town hall this Thursday. If you'd like to join me as an observer, you are welcome," he offered.

"I'd love that. Thank you." Taylor appreciated the chance to see how Joe approached his interviews.

A little over an hour later, Victoria's fiancé joined

them. She introduced Todd to everyone and Taylor immediately noticed that they seemed to be opposites. Todd was also very tall and was wearing a suit, with his tie loosened. He was very quiet and just smiled at Victoria as she chatted animatedly non-stop. Taylor supposed it was hard for him to get a word in edge-wise, but maybe he liked being more of a listener. Victoria was happy to brag on his behalf, too.

"Todd just closed the biggest sale in his real estate firm's history. A twenty-six million dollar waterfront estate."

Todd smiled. "Thanks, but it hasn't actually closed yet. We just had an accepted offer."

Victoria laughed. "It will though. I have no doubt. And we are going out to dinner tonight to celebrate."

"Where are you going?" Mary asked.

"Wherever Victoria wants," Todd said.

"I think maybe The Whitley. That seems like a good, special occasional place," Victoria said.

"I've never eaten there, but I've heard it's marvelous," Mary said wistfully.

"Oh, it is! Todd took me there last year on my birthday. Have you been there yet, Taylor?"

"No, not yet. Someday, maybe," Taylor said. She couldn't think of any upcoming special occasions that warranted a visit there, and she couldn't really afford to splurge like that just yet. She wanted to feel a little more secure in her job and build her savings up a bit before spending any more than was necessary.

After about an hour or so, people started leaving and eventually it was just Taylor, Mary, Joe and Blake left at the bar. Taylor finished the last sip of her glass of wine and was about to say goodnight when Blake suggested another round and some appetizers.

"Are you guys hungry at all? The wings and all the apps here are great. We could get a few things and share?"

"I'll stay for another, and some wings," Mary said.

"I'm ready for another beer," Joe agreed.

"How about you, Taylor?" Blake asked.

"Sure, why not."

Blake ordered the round of drinks and some wings, peel and eat shrimp and pineapple kielbasa bites. It was all delicious. Taylor mostly listened as the other three laughed and reminisced about their years of working together. It was interesting hearing about some of the stories they'd worked on.

"Daffodil weekend is coming up soon. Have you been here for that, Taylor?" Blake asked.

She shook her head. "No. I've heard about it though. There's a parade of old cars or something like that?"

He smiled. "Yes, it's a big deal here. Lots of people come over that weekend for the festivities. There is a parade of vintage automobiles and people plan elaborate picnics and line up along the parade route to watch, and eat and drink. It's a lot of fun, actually. Joe will be covering that for us, right?"

Joe almost spit out the beer he'd just taken a sip of. He grinned. "Sure, if you want my resignation on your desk."

Blake laughed and turned to Taylor. "Yeah, that's not really up Joe's alley. I was thinking you might find it fun to cover though, if you're interested?"

"I'd love to." It sounded like a great assignment to her. Though she was really up for just about anything.

"You'll enjoy that," Mary said. "And be sure to get a good look at some of the picnics. People go all out. Many either have them catered or even have a personal chef cooking right there on a portable grill."

"Wow. That sounds a bit much," Taylor said.

Blake laughed. "That's Nantucket for you. It really is a good time."

"Is your mother back on the island, Blake?" Mary asked. "I thought I saw her walking out of Stop and Shop the other day."

"Yes, she's back from Florida a little earlier than usual. My dad is still down there for a few more weeks. She wanted to come back and oversee getting the house ready for them. Or so she says."

Mary chuckled at that. "She's worried that you're still single, isn't she?"

Taylor thought she was kidding, but Blake nodded. "Yeah. I think she was more upset than any of us when Caroline dumped me. She's been trying to play match-maker from Florida, which of course is ridiculous. And I keep telling her I don't need her help."

"Her track record isn't great. Isn't she the one that introduced you to Caroline?" Joe said.

"She is," Blake confirmed.

"It's because you're the only single one left," Mary said.

Blake nodded. "Right. Blair got married five years ago and produced the first grandchild already, so you'd think I'd be off the hook."

"Is your mother retired too?" Taylor asked.

"She actually never worked. So there was nothing to retire from. But she keeps busy. She's always been involved with her church and volunteer organizations. And she and my father both love to golf."

"Are you a golfer, too?" Taylor had never tried it.

"Not as much as my parents. They are both in leagues and play all the time. I go out now and then. It's fun, when you have the time. Do you golf?"

"No, I've always thought it looked fun though."

"It can be. You should give it a try."

"Maybe I will over the summer. First, I have to learn how to needlepoint."

He laughed at that. "You signed up for Connie's class?"

She smiled. "I did. My friend Abby is going with me. It's something to do."

"Speaking of something to do. Trivia starts up again next Thursday at the Rose and Crown. Are you in, Blake?" Joe asked. "We could use a few more people. Emily and Jason from sales and Mary are up for it."

"Yes, I'm in." Blake turned to Taylor. "Do you want to join us? It's team trivia on Thursday nights and it's a lot of fun."

"I'd love that. I used to play with friends in Charleston. There's a bunch of teams and three winners at the end of the night, usually a gift card to use at the restaurant on the next visit."

"That's how they do it here, too. Even when we come in dead last, it's still a good time."

CHAPTER 11

Marley was having a wonderful Saturday. She'd gotten up early, and walked for a half hour along the beach. After that, she'd showered, then run into town to do some errands and grocery shop. After a quick lunch, she settled into her office and began work on a new consulting project. It was for someone she'd met at the conference, and it was a fascinating assignment that involved a lot of data analytics and researching the competitive marketplace.

She quickly lost herself in the work and several hours passed before she decided to take a break and make a cup of tea. It was about three in the afternoon and she planned to work for a few more hours before getting ready to go out to dinner with Mark. They had reservations at Keeper's, one of their favorite restaurants, and she was looking forward to seeing him. They normally saw each other during the week, but because of the conference, she'd been too busy.

She was just heading back to her office with a cup of Earl Grey green tea when her phone rang and she smiled when she saw it was Lisa.

"Hey Lisa, perfect timing. I just took a break." Marley settled back at her desk and glanced out the window. It was a sunny day, but windy, and the sea was choppy with frothy, white-capped waves.

"Have you had a chance to look at this week's paper yet?" Lisa's tone made Marley feel a bit uneasy.

"No, not yet. It's right here on my desk, though, in my pile of mail. What is it?"

"Look at page three."

Marley flipped open the paper and her jaw dropped. In the middle of the page there was a huge photo of her and Frank seemingly gazing into each other's eyes over cocktails, and the caption below said, "Reunited and it feels so good?"

"Oh, no! That's not what was going on at all."

"Read the article. It gets worse," Lisa said.

Marley read it and fumed. It was typical Frank. The interviewer, Victoria Carson, who Marley had never even heard of before, asked Frank a bunch of questions about his business which he was thrilled to answer and then she slipped in a question about Marley.

"You and your ex-wife seem to be getting along well. Any chance of a reconciliation?" To which Frank had replied, "My fingers are crossed and I'm optimistic, that's all I'll say."

"I hate to tell you, but it gets worse. Google your name or Frank's. It's been picked up by all the online media and is everywhere," Lisa said. "I'm so sorry. That must be so annoying."

Marley sighed. "It's exactly what I was afraid might happen if we went anywhere together. I didn't see any media at the event. Who is Victoria Carson? I'm not familiar with that name."

"She's new at the paper. Started a week before Taylor, Abby's friend that is staying here for a bit."

Marley held her breath as she typed her name and Frank's into the Google search bar. Sure enough, a flurry of stories popped up, all with that awful photo. She knew exactly when it was taken. It was when she and Frank had finished their sessions that first day and he offered to buy her a drink. He went to the bar and returned with cocktails for both of them. They spoke for all of about two minutes before they were surrounded by people Frank knew. It wasn't an intimate conversation by any means. But she knew that wasn't how it looked.

"I wonder if Mark has seen this yet?" Marley wondered. She knew it was inevitable that he would.

"He'll know there's nothing to it. Things are good with you two, right?" Lisa asked.

"Yes, they've been great. But he was a little apprehensive about me seeing Frank. I also told him that Frank wanted to get back together, but that it wasn't going to happen."

"Well, this doesn't look good. But I'm sure Mark will understand," Lisa said.

"I hope so. We have dinner plans tonight at Keeper's."

"Oh, I love that place. I'm sure it will be fine and you will both have a good laugh over it at dinner. Call me tomorrow."

"I will." Marley hoped Lisa was right. Mark was from Nantucket. He wasn't used to the craziness of the media. Or of how things were often misrepresented and presented as truth. It was one thing Marley had been glad to get away from when she left the company. She knew there were many wonderful reporters, but there were also story chasers that didn't particularly care about context or making sure everything was true before running with juicy gossip.

Marley returned to her work, but found it difficult to focus. After a while, she gave up and decided to do laundry instead and some cleaning around the house that she'd put off. She was a little surprised that Mark hadn't called to check in. He usually did when they had plans just to touch base. Just as she was about to head upstairs and get ready, the phone rang and it was Mark.

"Hey there! I was just heading upstairs to get changed. How was your day?"

He was quiet for a moment. "I've had better. I picked up a copy of the Nantucket paper while I was out and about and saw your picture. The article surprised me." His tone was somewhat cold and distant.

"Mark, that's nonsense. Frank and I are not getting back together."

"Well, you looked pretty cozy in that picture. And you said he wanted to talk to you about it. Did you have him over to your house?"

"I did. Because we didn't want to be seen in public. But I told him in no uncertain terms that getting back together wasn't going to happen."

"Right. He seemed pretty set on it in that article, though. And the two of you looked like you were on a date."

Marley sighed. "It's not at all how it looked. We talked for all of two minutes before a crowd joined us. Frank just bought me a drink, and we caught up a little. That's all. There's nothing to be jealous about."

"I'm not jealous. I just don't want to be wasting my time." He paused for a moment. "I think maybe we should take a break. You come from a very different background than I do. Maybe the high-profile world of high tech is where you belong, not here, with me. Maybe you'll be happier if you go back to that world, and to Frank."

Marley suddenly felt infuriated. Mark hadn't listened to her at all. "Who are you to tell me what is going to make me happy? I bought a house on Nantucket. This is where I want to be. And how many times do I have to tell you that I'm not getting back with Frank? Maybe you're right, though. Right now, a break seems like a good idea. Good night, Mark." Marley hung up without even waiting for a response. She was so annoyed at the situation, at Frank and at Mark.

So, instead of going to one of her favorite restaurants with her boyfriend, Marley ordered a pizza to be delivered, went and changed into her oldest, softest sweats and poured herself a big glass of cabernet. She'd eat her fill of pizza, flop in front of the TV and see if she could lose herself in a romantic comedy and, hopefully, tomorrow would be a better day.

———————

TAYLOR WAS THE FIRST PERSON IN THE NEWSROOM ON Monday. Mary was just settling in at the front desk when Taylor walked through the door at a quarter to nine. She'd eaten a quick breakfast at the Inn and visited with Lisa and Rhett before heading into work. It was the first time she could remember actually looking forward to the beginning of a new workweek.

"Good morning! I just started a pot of coffee in the kitchen. Should be ready any minute if you want to help yourself," Mary said.

"Thank you. Did you have a good weekend?"

Mary beamed. "I did. My sister came to visit, which is always fun. How about you?"

Taylor grinned. "I still feel like I'm playing tourist here, so it was very fun. I did some shopping downtown and went out to dinner with friends." Abby and Jeff got a sitter Saturday night, and they went out with Abby's brother Chase and his wife, Beth, to The Gaslight and stayed after dinner to listen to some live music. Taylor had spent Sunday relaxing, and catching up on some reading.

She grabbed a half-cup of coffee and settled at her desk. Ten minutes later, Blake, Joe and Victoria walked in and it was like someone flipped an energy switch. The room went from quiet to electric, just like that, as cell phones started ringing, and both Joe and Victoria jumped on calls as Emily in sales and Bill from graphics raced over to get Blake's attention first.

"Blake, I have a client issue.." Emily began.

"Blake, this is urgent. We need to call a technician asap.." Bill said.

Blake glanced at Taylor and grinned. "Typical Monday morning around here." He gestured for Emily and Bill to follow him to his office.

Twenty minutes later, Victoria finished her call, turned around and said hello to Taylor.

"Good morning! How was your weekend?"

"Fun. A bunch of us went to The Gaslight Saturday night. How was your celebration dinner at The Whitley?"

"Amazing. We did the tasting menu, and the courses kept coming and they were all so good. And of course there were wines to match each one."

"Of course."

"Todd actually surprised me by renting us a room for the night there, too. A suite with a fireplace. So, after dinner we didn't have far to go. It was really incredible."

"Wow, that sounds wonderful."

Victoria grinned. "It was. And yesterday I saw that my article on The Attic and Frank and Marley Higgins went viral! It got picked up by the national media, and it's everywhere."

Taylor hesitated. Lisa had filled her in on how upset Marley was about that article. "Congratulations. But, what do you do when something you run isn't quite true?"

Victoria looked confused. "What do you mean, not true? I talked to Frank himself."

"Yes. But you didn't talk to Marley and they are not back together. In fact, that article upset Marley's boyfriend so much that he broke up with her. She's not happy at all."

Victoria frowned. "Oh. Frank made it seem like they were getting back together. I just assumed she felt the same."

"Victoria, you should know better than to assume anything. Why didn't you interview Marley too if they were both there?" Blake had walked up and caught the tail end of their conversation. Taylor hadn't even heard him come up behind her.

"I tried to talk to her first, but couldn't get her alone. She was always in a conversation with someone. Frank didn't actually say they were back together, just that he hoped it would happen. So, I don't see that I did anything wrong," Victoria said. She was on the defensive now and annoyed that her story wasn't accurate.

Blake thought for a moment. "That's true. It's unfortunate that you weren't able to confirm with Marley, but Frank did say what was true, for him. However, I don't blame Marley for being upset, especially as this did go viral. Here's what I want you to do. Call Marley and see if she'll talk to you now and tell her you want to set the record straight. This will give us another follow-up article. And maybe it will go viral too, or not. But at least it will be in our local paper and I suspect that's what Marley cares about the most."

"Okay, I'm on it. I'll call her now." Victoria spun around in her chair and jumped on the internet to get Marley's phone number.

Taylor turned her attention back to her own work. She was glad, for Marley's sake, that there would be a follow-up piece. She didn't know Marley, but she was such a good friend of Lisa's and it sounded like a frustrating situation. Bad enough to have something printed that wasn't true, but to then have someone else believe it would be awful. It made her realize how important it was to ensure that any story she wrote was accurate.

CHAPTER 12

For the next few days, Rhett paid closer attention to everything going on in his restaurant. Normally he was attuned to the general rhythm and jumped in to help wherever it was needed — focusing on servers that were in the weeds and needed an order delivered to a table or customers that were looking around as if trying to find their server. He helped with seating people when it got busy at the hostess stand and he spent quite a bit of time over by the bar, schmoozing with regulars who stopped in for a drink before dinner. He was used to noticing people and customers, not focusing on the small details of how his employees did their jobs.

And even with that focus turned up a notch, he didn't notice anything out of the ordinary until Thursday when one of the Winkleton twins was behind the bar. They both graduated from college in December and had spent two years working for him during summers and breaks.

Aidan and Alex were identical twins, and the only way anyone could tell them apart was a small shark tattoo on Aidan's wrist. Otherwise, it was like looking in a mirror— impossible to tell who was who.

Aidan worked in the kitchen as a line cook and Alex, the more outgoing of the two, was behind the bar. They were well liked by everyone and Rhett had always found them dependable and hard-working. So, at first, he was inclined to think his eyes were playing tricks on him.

Rhett first noticed something was up when he was chatting with two of his favorite regulars, the Johnsons. Lou and Betty came in for dinner almost every Thursday night without fail and had a cocktail at the bar before sitting down at a table. He was mid-conversation with them when out of the corner of his eye he noticed Alex take an order for two top shelf martinis, make the drinks, deliver them to the customers, take cash and make change from the register. All of which was normal, except that Alex didn't seem to ring the drinks in.

At least Rhett didn't think that he did. At the end of the night, the bartenders would normally close out their registers, count the money and pay themselves tips owed from credit cards. They left the cash drawer with the same amount it started with and put the night's profits and credit card slips in a bank deposit bag. Rhett knew it would be a simple thing to pocket the cash on orders that were never run in.

He hated to think that Alex might be doing that, though. Maybe he'd missed seeing Alex ring the drinks in. Rhett watched when he could for the rest of the evening and didn't notice it happening again, but he wasn't at the bar all night.

Later that night, around eleven o'clock, he was home and in bed with Lisa. They were settling in for the night and Lisa was planning to read for a bit before going to sleep. Usually, Rhett did the same or watched TV. Tonight, he watched his iPad. He'd told Lisa what he thought he saw, and she was curious to know if the cameras could confirm what he thought he'd seen. He was going through the footage, but so far, hadn't seen anything unusual. Until he did.

"Lisa, check this out. This clip shows Alex taking two twenties and opening the register to make change and not ringing anything in. My eyes weren't playing tricks on me."

Lisa watched the clip and shook her head. "I'm sorry. That is disappointing. He seemed like such a nice kid."

"He is. Charming too and a good bartender. Too bad he's a thief. Now I need to find a new bartender."

"Was it just the one time? Maybe it was an innocent mistake," Lisa said.

"Hmm. Possibly. I'll keep looking. If it wasn't a mistake, he's probably doing it more than once a night."

Rhett spent the next half hour going through more of the tape, hoping he wouldn't find anything else and that it was just a one-off, a hopefully innocent mistake. But it didn't take long before he found five more instances.

"He's giving himself a nice bonus out of my pocket," Rhett said in disgust.

"I'm sorry. So what will you do about it?" Lisa asked.

"I've been thinking about that. He works tomorrow night. I'm pretty sure he's doing this regularly, but I'll watch tomorrow night and hopefully notice it again. And at the end of the night, I'll surprise him by grabbing the cash register and doing the checkout myself. The tape will be running as well, so if I find extra cash, which I'm sure I will, I'll have the tape to show how it happened."

"Will you call the police? Or just fire him?"

Rhett sighed. "I'll have to call the police. If I just fire him, he'll go somewhere else and do it again. At least with it on record, restaurants will think twice about hiring him to handle their cash."

"Well, I'm glad you at least know what's going on."

Rhett's iPad dinged, announcing a new video from the security camera.

"What's that?" Lisa asked.

"I'm not sure. It's from the back door camera." Rhett clicked on the video and he and Lisa both watched as Alex held the back door open while his brother Aidan carried out two boxes of food. One of chicken breasts and one of steaks.

"Wow. What are they doing with that, do you think?" Lisa asked.

Suddenly, it all made sense. "Aidan and Alex are often the last people there to close the bar and the kitchen. Someone mentioned recently that Aidan does a little catering on the side. Looks like we know where he's getting his supplies."

"That's awful. Now you have to fire both of them," Lisa said.

"Not to mention that I'm going to be short an experienced line cook and bartender now. The only good thing is that this happened in March instead of July."

"That's very true. Good luck with it tomorrow. That's not going to be a pleasant conversation," Lisa said.

"No, it's not," Rhett agreed. He was already dreading the next night, but knew it had to be dealt with. And everyone in the restaurant needed to be informed and know that he wasn't going to put up with anything like that happening again.

THE WINKLETON TWINS DIDN'T MAKE IT EASY FOR HIM. The next night Rhett went into work with a heavy heart, dreading what he needed to do.

Alex smiled when he saw him and chatted as if they were good friends.

"What do you think of the Red Sox's chances this year? I think the team is looking good. Aidan and I are hoping to get tickets to opening day."

It was hard for Rhett to digest that these likable kids that had worked for him for so long could be ripping him off. After chatting with him for a few minutes, Alex went off to get his bar ready for the night, and Rhett paid close attention to everything that evening. He hoped he'd see Alex scamming drinks early, and it would make him feel a little better about firing him at the end of the night.

But by a quarter to ten, and the restaurant closing in fifteen minutes, Rhett hadn't seen Alex make one wrong move. He didn't want to make a big to-do about counting the cash register if it would be the one night Alex didn't do anything wrong. So he went into his office and pulled out his iPad to look at the video clips taken through the evening. Rhett hadn't been at the bar the entire night. He'd roamed around as usual and hopefully Alex chose those times to not use the register.

Sure enough, a quick scroll through less than half of the clips showed six times Alex took cash and didn't ring the drinks in. Rhett had what he needed. He went back into the dining room, chatted with Elsa for a minute at the hostess stand, and checked with Nora, his manager, who was adjusting the schedule for a server that wanted to switch shifts. When she was finished, he pulled her aside and told her what was going on and asked her to stay with him when he brought Alex into his office. He wanted to make sure he did this properly with a witness. He also called David, one of the Nantucket cops that he knew, and gave him a heads up. David asked him to shoot him a text when he was ready for him to come by.

Rhett went back into the dining room and strolled over to the bar. The last guest was paying his tab with a credit card. Alex ran it through the machine and handed it back to the customer. As soon as he walked away, Rhett stepped behind the bar and went to the register. He ran the day's receipts and pulled the drawer out of the machine. Alex looked confused. "I haven't closed that out yet. I was just about to do it," he said.

"No worries. I'm going to handle it tonight. Why don't you come watch, though. I've recently instituted some new security measures. Nora is going to sit in on this too."

Alex just stared at him, unsure what to make of the situation. And then followed Rhett and Nora to Rhett's office. They both sat in the two chairs facing Rhett's desk, while Rhett settled in his chair, set the cash drawer down, got out his calculator, and quickly counted up the cash and then the credit card slips. It didn't take long.

When he finished, there was close to $200 in credit card tips, which he handed to Alex. Plus the cash in the jar by the machine, which Rhett didn't touch. That was also all Alex's. The drawer was over by a hundred and twenty dollars. Rhett sighed. And wondered how long Alex had been doing this for. He looked up and addressed Alex, who looked very uncomfortable in his chair.

"The drawer is over by a hundred and twenty dollars. Do you have any idea why that might be?" Rhett asked calmly.

Alex stayed silent for a long moment, then shrugged his shoulders. "I have no idea. It must have been over from the beginning."

Rhett glanced at Nora, who shook her head. "It wasn't. I counted it myself after Rhett gave it to me and it was the same amount it always is."

"And I counted it before she took it. So, I'll ask again, why is the drawer over, Alex?"

"Must be a mistake of some sort." He grinned. "That's better than being short though, right?"

"Not quite. It seems that when you work behind the bar, this happens. And it's not better than being short because the end result is the same—I'm the one that ends up short, when you pocket the extra cash."

"I would never do that!" Alex protested.

Rhett sent a quick text to David, then opened his iPad and found one of the incriminating videos and hit play. He turned it around and set it in front of Alex. He watched for a moment, then turned pale.

"Nora, could you please ask Aidan to come in here too?"

She left and returned a moment later with Alex's brother. She gestured for Aidan to take a seat while she remained standing. He sat and glanced at his brother with a puzzled expression. Alex couldn't look at any of them. He stared at the floor and his right foot was moving back and forth.

Rhett found the video from the night before ofAidan leaving with the two cases of food. Before he hit play, he addressed the two boys.

"I've been trying to figure out for a few weeks now why our numbers seem off. We're busy, but the cash is low and we're going through food faster. Something wasn't adding up. I finally figured out what was going on, though. Alex was skimming from the bar, keeping cash and not ringing the drinks up. AndAidan, you were stealing food from the walk-in."

"I would never do that!" Aidan immediately protested.

"But you did." Rhett hit play on the iPad and handed it toAidan. "I had some security cameras installed, and that helped us figure out what was going on. This footage was from last night. I believe that's a box of chicken and filet mignons that you took, with your brother's help."

Aidan set the iPad down and glanced nervously at his brother, who just looked miserable.

"Look, I'm really sorry. It was a one-time thing. I swear it will never happen again,"Aidan said.

"I'm afraid I don't believe that for a minute. You're both fired, effective immediately. What I don't under-stand, though, is how you could do it? I trusted both of you and thought you were good kids. How could you steal from me?"

"We didn't think you'd miss it,"Aidan said. "Food is expensive, and I've been trying to get a catering business started. I know it was wrong. Like I said, it won't happen again."

"I'm sorry, too," Alex said. "I didn't think it was a big deal, really. It was just a few drinks here and there."

Rhett shook his head in disgust and disappointment as his friend Dave, the police officer, knocked on the door.

"Are these the two you told me about?" Dave asked.

Rhett nodded. "Yes, and there're loads of video evidence on my iPad." He replayed the video of the two brothers carrying out the cases of food.

Dave watched it and handed the iPad back to Rhett. "Can you email those videos to me?"

"Sure thing."

Dave turned to Alex and Aidan. "Please come with me gentlemen, we need to head down to the station to get you both processed."

Alex looked horrified and annoyed. "You're not just firing us? You're pressing charges too?"

Aidan stood and looked confused. "Are we being arrested?"

Dave smiled, "You are. Come along with me."

Alex glared at Rhett. "I can't believe you're pressing charges."

"It doesn't give me any pleasure, believe me. But I couldn't live with myself if I just fired you and then you went and did this somewhere else. Which I think we both know you would."

Alex and Aidan had no response to that and were silent as they followed Dave to the police car.

As soon as they were gone, Rhett sighed and looked at Nora. "Well, that's something I hope I never have to do again. Now let's go tell the rest of the staff what happened."

CHAPTER 13

As promised, Joe took Taylor with him for his Thursday afternoon interview at town hall. He was meeting with the chairman of one of the town boards and there were several issues Joe wanted to cover a few issues that residents were concerned about and that were under discussion by the board or had recently been voted on.

Joe introduced her to the chairman and Taylor sat silently observing and taking notes on a yellow legal pad as Joe began the interview. She noticed that Joe didn't jump into asking questions right away. Instead, he and the chairman had a seemingly irrelevant conversation punctuated with laughter, about what they did over the weekend, where the best fishing was and how the Red Sox's chances looked for the upcoming season. Taylor also noticed that by the time Joe got around to asking his first question, the chairman was more relaxed.

They spent about an hour at town hall. After their

meeting, Joe introduced Taylor to a few other people they ran into in the hallways. The names went in one ear and out the other, but she was impressed by how Joe knew just about everyone there and had in-depth conversations with all of them. He was clearly on top of all the local government issues. His interview with the chairman had been fascinating, even though Taylor wasn't up to speed on all the issues they discussed.

It was valuable to see how Joe approached asking his questions, how he started with a broad easy one first and then drilled down to more specifics. She realized that she still had so much to learn about how to do her job well. And what she'd learned today would help in future interviews. She wondered if Victoria might let her tag along on one of her upcoming interviews. It would be interesting to compare their styles. Hopefully Victoria would find the request flattering and not too annoying.

"So what did you think?" Joe asked once they were in his car and on their way back to the newspaper.

"It was awesome. Thank you so much for letting me join you. I learned a lot. Especially how you spend time at the beginning just talking before diving into the actual interview."

He nodded, seemingly pleased by the compliment. "Yeah, that was one of the first things I learned years ago. People tend to open up more if they like you or even just feel like they know you a bit and having a conversation about anything other than what you are there to talk about kind of breaks the ice."

When they got back to the newsroom, Victoria was

just getting off a call and raised her eyebrows when she saw Taylor and Joe walk in together.

"Joe let me tag along on an interview at town hall," Taylor said. "It was really helpful to see how he approaches things. I'm still pretty new at this," she admitted.

Victoria glanced at her phone for a minute, then looked up. "I have an interview next Monday that might be fun for you if you're interested in joining me. I'm interviewing Mia, a local wedding planner I am actually using for my wedding next year, for a piece on extravagant over-the-top weddings on Nantucket."

"I'd love to. Thank you."

AT A QUARTER TO FIVE, BLAKE WALKED OVER TO THEIR desks. "Are both of you coming to trivia tonight? We need all the help we can get."

Victoria made a face. "I am not really into trivia. Have fun though."

Blake laughed. "One of these weeks we will wear you down and you'll be surprised how much fun it is."

"Maybe, but I wouldn't hold your breath on that." Victoria smiled as she turned back to her computer to shut it down for the day.

"What about you, Taylor? You still up for joining us?" Blake looked hopeful.

"Yes, I'm in." Unlike Victoria, Taylor loved going to trivia. It was just a fun night out and everyone always had different topics they tended to do well with. Taylor never seemed to know the geography or history questions, but did well on literature, movies, and sometimes science. And even when her team lost totally, it was still a lot of fun.

Five of them, Taylor, Blake, Joe, Mary, and Emily, walked the short distance to the Rose and Crown, the restaurant/pub. Trivia started at six, and they all ordered food and drinks first. The menu was typical for a casual pub with lots of sandwiches, burgers, fried food and appetizers like nachos, wings, and fried calamari. They ordered a few appetizers for the table and a round of cocktails. Taylor hadn't had a burger in a while and saw one go by that looked delicious, so she ordered that for her main meal.

The conversation around the table was lively, and they laughed and chatted as they ate. Just as they were finishing up their meals, the trivia host came around to their table and dropped off a score sheet, pencil, and answer pads. He seemed to know everyone and put everything in front of Blake.

"Blake always keeps score," Mary said. She was sitting on Taylor's right and Blake was on her left.

Blake looked around the table. "Keep the team name the same?" Everyone nodded.

"What's the name?" Taylor asked.

Blake grinned. "Nantucket News. Original, huh?"

She laughed. "Seems fitting."

Trivia lasted for the next two hours and it was a good time. Their team was doing well—out of eleven teams, they were in second place when they got to the final question of the night. Blake and Joe were great at the geography, sports and history questions, while Emily, like Taylor, was also good with entertainment and English-related ones and Mary knew all the Seinfeld and food questions. But on the final question almost anyone could win as they could bet up to all of their points and with team trivia, whoever won the final trivia question often won it all.

"Okay, the final question category is the TV show Friends. Let me know your final wagers," the trivia host announced.

Blake looked around the table. "How good do we feel about our chances with Friends? I know we've all seen the show, but there were ten seasons. That's a lot to remember. I always think I know Seinfeld, but I never know the answers, though luckily Mary usually does."

"I can guarantee that I will not know that answer," Joe stated.

"I've seen most of the episodes. But it has been a while," Emily said.

"I don't know Friends as well as I know Seinfeld," Mary said.

"I feel so-so about it." Blake didn't look confident about his chances.

"I actually feel pretty good about it," Taylor said. "I've been binge watching it again over the past few months."

"All right. Let's go for it then," Blake said. "We'll bet all but one point, so if everyone misses it, we still have a chance." He handed their wager slip to Owen, the trivia host, when he came by to collect them and a moment later Owen announced the final question.

"Ross gets suspended from the museum because of anger management issues. Why was he angry?"

Blake looked around the table. "I don't have a clue. Anyone?" They all shook their heads.

"I know I've seen that one," Emily said. "But I can't remember what it was."

Taylor breathed a sigh of relief. She would have felt awful if she hadn't known the answer after saying she felt good about the category. She grinned, leaned in and spoke softly so no one beyond their table could hear, "He was mad that someone ate his sandwich."

Emily laughed. "Yes! That was it. Someone took it out of the refrigerator and it was labeled with his name, too. He was furious."

Blake wrote it down and walked the slip over to the trivia host. A few minutes later, he announced the answer and the top three winners.

"And in first place, with a $25 gift card to use on a future visit, congratulations to Nantucket News!"

The trivia host handed the gift card to Blake, who then gave it to Taylor. "Why don't you hold on to it for safe-keeping and we'll use it next time we play?"

"Sure." Taylor tucked it into an inside pocket of her purse.

Their waitress dropped off their check, and they all chipped in, then left and walked back to the paper and their cars.

"So, what did you think, Taylor? You have to come

next week, you know, since you have the gift card," Blake teased her.

She laughed. "It was great. And I look forward to it." She felt like she was part of the team now, and it was fun to have co-workers to play trivia or have after-work drinks with. They all got along well. Joe was a lot of fun when he was outside of work and not so focused. Emily was close to her age, and they'd chatted a bit during the night and found out they liked some of the same shows, and Mary was funny and the most competitive one, which had surprised Taylor at first.

Blake was growing on her more and more, too. And she had to remind herself that he was her boss. She couldn't like him too much. But he was easy to like and sitting so close to him, she couldn't help but notice that the cologne he wore smelled so good. Now and then she caught a faint whiff of it.

It didn't take long to walk back and everyone said goodnight and went on their way. Blake didn't have far to go as he lived above the paper.

He smiled her way as he turned to go. "Night Taylor. See you in the am."

"Goodnight, Blake."

When she reached her car, she glanced back at the building and saw a light come on upstairs. She found herself wondering if Blake was dating anyone. And then immediately pushed the thought out of her mind. Having a crush on her boss was definitely not a good idea.

CHAPTER 14

L isa added another pinch of rosemary to the oversized crock pot full of simmering short ribs. She gave it all a big stir and took a tiny taste. It was just right. She'd finally perfected her short ribs recipe after making them just about every possible way under the sun.

Her final recipe was simple but rich and delicious, with lots of wine, mushrooms, demi-glace and other spices. She made a bigger batch than usual because she was expecting a larger crowd today for Sunday dinner. All the kids and their significant others were coming and, of course, her grandchildren too.

It was almost six, and she knew they'd be arriving any minute. Kate and Abby and their families would be first, followed by Chase and Beth, and the last to arrive, always fashionably late, would be Kristen and Tyler.

"Are you ready for a glass?" Rhett asked as he opened a new bottle of cabernet.

She smiled. "Do you really need to ask?"

He chuckled and took two glasses out of the cupboard while Lisa got out the chilled bowl of pimento cheese spread she'd made earlier. It was a new recipe, and she wanted to get the kids' opinion on it. She set it in the middle of the kitchen island as everyone always gathered in the kitchen before settling down to eat. She opened a box of crackers and poured them onto a plate by the cheese and found a good knife for spreading and made a cracker up for Rhett.

"Try this." She handed him the cracker heavily topped with the spread, which was a mix of hand shredded cheddar, cream cheese, mayo, pimentos and a few seasonings. Rhett popped it in his mouth and immediately gave her the thumbs up. She made one for herself too as the front door opened and she heard Kate and Abby's voices.

"Mom, that smells amazing," Kate said, as she walked into the kitchen. "Short ribs?"

Lisa smiled. "Yes, and I think I've finally settled on a recipe. Try the cheese spread though and let me know what you think."

Kate laughed. "Your short ribs are always amazing." She poured herself a glass of wine and helped herself to some of the cheese and crackers. "Oh, this is really good, too. It has an unexpected kick to it. What is that?"

"Worcestershire and a dash of hot sauce." Lisa looked around the room.

"Where are my grandbabies?" It was too quiet. She only heard adult voices.

"They fell asleep in their car seats," Kate said. They were sound asleep still when Jack carried them in. But I'm sure that won't last long."

"Grammy!" Lisa's heart melted as Natalie ran over to her and demanded a hug. Abby was right behind her. Lisa picked her up and gave her a hug and a kiss.

"Someone had a long nap this afternoon, so she is wide awake now," Abby said. "Mommy is ready for a glass of wine."

Lisa laughed. "Help yourself, Rhett just opened a bottle of cabernet."

A few minutes later, Chase and Beth arrived and joined them in the kitchen. Beth stayed to chat while Chase gave Lisa a hug hello, grabbed a beer, and joined the guys in the living room. Lisa could faintly hear Rhett telling them about what had happened at the restaurant. Lisa had filled the girls in the day before when they came for breakfast. Well, other than Kristen.

She'd spent the weekend in Boston with Tyler. But they were taking the two o'clock ferry home, so Kristen said they'd be back in plenty of time to join them. It was rare that everyone was available for Sunday dinner on the same day, but Lisa loved when it worked out and all the people she loved were under her roof.

At ten after six, Lisa heard the front door open again and a minute later, Kristen and Tyler walked into the room. Lisa went to give her daughter a hug and stopped short when she noticed the huge diamond engagement ring on Kristen's finger.

Kristen noticed where Lisa's eyes went and laughed.

Lisa couldn't remember the last time she'd seen her daughter look so happy. Kristen was the quiet, reserved one and now she was beaming and Tyler looked just as pleased.

"I see congratulations are in order," Lisa said as she pulled Kristen in for a hug.

"Can you believe it?" Kristen still seemed to be in a bit of a daze.

Kate and Abby came rushing over. "You got engaged!" Abby said.

"Let's see the ring," Kate said. "And congratulations!"

Kristen held her hand up so they could all admire it. It was a beautiful ring, princess cut with smaller diamonds on either side in a platinum setting.

"That's huge," Abby said. "It's gorgeous."

"It's three carats. I told Tyler it was too extravagant, but he said when he saw it, he knew it was the one."

Lisa saw that Tyler had already escaped the room and joined the guys.

"It's beautiful, Kristen. I'm so happy for you," Lisa said.

"So, how did he do it?" Kate asked. "Tell us everything."

Abby poured Kristen a glass of wine and handed it to her. "Okay, sit down and relax and then, like Kate said, we need to hear every detail."

Kristen laughed and settled herself on one of the bar stools at the island, and they all gathered around her.

"So, I really had no idea he was planning this. I thought we were just going to have a fun weekend in

Boston celebrating Tyler finishing his newest book. TheAirbnb we stayed at was adorable. It was right on Charles Street, small but cozy, and it was just a block from the cutest French restaurant. We had reservations there last night, and that's where Tyler proposed."

"Was it Ma Maison?" Abby asked.

"Yes! That was it. I couldn't remember the name. It was such a cute place, small and romantic. The food was amazing. Tyler waited until we were on dessert. We were sharing a strawberry baked Alaska, when the waiter brought over a bottle of champagne which I thought was a little strange, but Tyler said it went well with the dessert and we had something to celebrate. I thought he was talking about his book. But then, he dropped to one knee and asked me to marry him!"

"I'm so happy for you, honey. You and Tyler really seem great together," Lisa said. She'd had her concerns initially, but Kristen had handled Tyler's relapse well and they both seemed so well suited, happy, and just right together.

"Thank you. I knew it was going to happen at some point. We'd talked about it a few times, but it felt further in the future. He really surprised me." She still seemed dazed and kept looking at her ring.

"Kristen, I am thrilled for you. I've always thought he was perfect for you," Kate said.

Kristen's eyes welled up as she hugged her sister. "You did!"

Abby hugged her next. "So awesome. Congratulations."

Beth offered her congratulations too, and a hug.

Lisa went and checked on the mashed potatoes that were warming in the oven. They looked all set.

"Well, everything is ready if you all want to sit down to eat."

They made their way in to the dining room and Kate went to check on the twins who were stirring. She got them settled with bottles and then helped Lisa carry plates of food to the table.

The conversation was lively as they ate and drank. Lisa and Rhett sat on opposite ends of the table and he caught her eye a few times and smiled. Lisa was really in her glory with everyone around her, enjoying food that she'd made for them. They shared how their week had gone and caught each other up on anything new in their lives.

"Mom, did I tell you I'm going to start a needlepoint class this week with Taylor? She did a story on the new shop and there's a beginners' class and it sounds kind of fun," Abby said.

"Oh, you'll love that. You've always enjoyed crafty stuff," Lisa said. "I went through a needlepoint phase about ten years ago. It is fun. Relaxing too."

"Which night is the class?" Beth asked. She and Abby were close friends.

"Tuesday night. Do you want to come with us?"

"I might. If you think there's room?"

"Call the shop tomorrow. The more the merrier!"

CHAPTER 15

Marley felt out of sorts all week, since her conversation with Mark on Saturday. She'd wallowed Saturday night, then on Sunday went for a long walk on the beach with Lisa, who advised her to wait it out and if it was meant to be with Mark, he'd come to his senses.

What bothered her the most was that he didn't seem to trust her or believe her when she said there was nothing there with Frank. There was nothing worse than being blamed for something you didn't do. It hurt, and it was disappointing. She expected better from him.

As the week went on, she alternated from missing him to feeling really annoyed. How could he ruin what had been such a good thing? She tried to focus on work and she had plenty of it, so that helped. But as the weekend drew near, she started feeling sad again. She and Mark usually saw each other at least once or twice during the week and always on the weekend. She could keep busy with work, but she'd rather do something fun.

And the last thing she felt like doing was going on a date with someone else. She'd never found dating fun, especially first dates, and she dreaded the thought of starting over again. She wasn't in any hurry for that. If things were truly over with Mark, then she would just focus on work again and enjoying Nantucket and maybe get out and join a new club or take a class, just to keep busy.

She didn't hear from Mark all week. She'd hoped he'd call after a day or two to apologize and say he overreacted, but he didn't. But late Friday afternoon, just as she was mentally preparing herself for a long, depressingly alone weekend, a gorgeous bouquet of white orchids arrived and a note from Mark that said, "I'm so sorry. Forgive me?"

Marley breathed a sigh of relief. She was glad to hear from him before the Saturday issue of the paper released. Victoria Carson had called earlier in the week and wanted to get her side of the story and she was happy to set her straight and confirm that there was no reunion happening with Frank. She'd hoped that would prove to Mark that she'd been telling the truth. But she was also annoyed that he would need that before getting in touch.

So, she was glad that he'd reached out before seeing the paper. It showed that there was hope for them. That he realized he could trust her, and hopefully he'd missed her as much as she'd missed him.

She was still frustrated that it had happened at all, so

she didn't call him to thank him for the flowers until the next morning. Let him think she was busy and out with friends or even a date Friday night—not that she would have ever, but she didn't mind letting him stew a little after what he'd done.

He didn't need to know that she'd had a date with her good friends Ben and Jerry, got into her pajamas right after dinner and spent the night binging old movies. She called him around eleven the next day and he picked up on the first ring.

"Marley? It's good to hear your voice. I missed you."

"Thank you for the flowers. They're lovely."

"This was a rotten week for me. I missed you and I worried that I'd blown it. I should have never questioned you."

"I missed you too. And I agree. You should have trusted me."

"Do you forgive me? I'd love to take you out tonight to make up for it. If you're free?"

"Yes, I forgive you. And I'd like that."

"We'll go anywhere you want. Just name the place."

Marley thought for a moment. "How about Ventuno's? Italian might be nice."

"Perfect. I'll make a reservation for seven and come by a little before to get you, if that works?"

"It does. I'll see you then." Marley smiled as she ended the call and leaned in for a sniff of the orchids, which smelled heavenly.

MARK CAME BY A LITTLE AFTER SIX THIRTY AND MARLEY was ready for him. She wore her favorite cashmere sweater in a pretty shade of aqua blue and her nicest pair of black dress pants. Mark looked handsome in a pinstriped button-down shirt and a blue tweed blazer.

"You look beautiful," he said as soon as he saw her. He seemed a little nervous.

"Thank you. You look nice too, I like your blazer." She grabbed her coat and purse and followed him to his truck. The ride to the restaurant didn't take long, and their table was ready for them when they arrived.

They took a look at the wine menu and chose a Sangiovese from Tuscany that sounded good. Marley ordered the linguine with white clam sauce and Mark got the ribeye steak. They split an appetizer that the restaurant was famous for, ricotta toast with homemade ricotta, drizzled with honey.

Everything was delicious, and as they sipped their wine and nibbled on the ricotta toast, Mark apologized again.

"I saw the paper this afternoon with the article correcting the earlier one. I'm glad they set that straight and spoke to you. I'm also glad I came to my senses before seeing the paper. I didn't need that to know I'd misjudged you."

"I'm glad too. That's what hurt the most, that you didn't believe me. I'd thought we were further along and that there was more trust there. So, it was disappointing."

Mark ran a hand through his hair and she could see in his eyes that he felt awful.

"I think I was just scared. Things were going so well with us. It's all been so easy. I think I almost didn't trust it. Not that I didn't trust you. I think it was my own doubts and worries that this was too good to be true. When I saw that picture, I just overreacted, plain and simple. It won't happen again."

Marley reached out and put her hand on his. "I think what we have is pretty special, too. And you don't ever have to worry about me."

Mark smiled and gave her hand a squeeze. "I know that now. I really missed you this week. I don't want to go that long without seeing you again if I can help it. There's something else I realized this week, Marley—I love you."

Marley looked at the man sitting across from her. Mark had come along out of the blue, when she'd least expected it and he was such a big part of her life now, that she couldn't imagine him not in it. Their relationship had been so easy, first as clients and friends and then a natural shift into a romance that took them both by surprise but in a wonderful way.

She felt a rush of happiness at his words. "I feel the same. I love you, too."

CHAPTER 16

"I'm really not in the mood to go out tonight," Abby said.

It was Tuesday night, and they'd just finished eating dinner. Jeff had already rinsed the dirty dishes and Abby loaded them into the dishwasher. Natalie was in the other room playing with her favorite doll. Jeff walked behind her and started massaging her shoulders.

"I think you should go. It will be good for you to be out with your friends and get your mind off of it. Tell them what's going on. It might help."

She nodded. "You're right. I will. I just thought it would be easier this time, you know? I guess that was silly of me. It's not like it was easy last time."

Jeff dug in a little deeper and it felt so good. Abby could feel the tension dissolving.

"It will happen for us again. We just need to relax and focus on something else."

Abby smiled. "Easier said than done. But I will try.

And I will go tonight. We're going to learn how to needle-point Christmas ornaments."

"Yes, you can't miss that." Jeff pulled her in for a reassuring kiss and she went off to get ready to meet the girls at the needlepoint shop.

BETH AND TAYLOR WERE ALREADY THERE WHEN ABBY arrived. They were sitting at a big round table that had a pile of supplies in the center. She slid into the empty chair between them. So far, they were the only ones there. But there were a few other women browsing in the shop. The class didn't start for ten more minutes still.

"If we finish early enough, do you want to grab coffee and dessert after?" Beth asked.

"I'd love to." Abby really did want to talk to the girls about what she was going through and didn't want to do it in front of a table full of strangers.

"That sounds good to me, too," Taylor said.

A few minutes later several more women and one man drifted in and took seats at the table. By six o'clock sharp, nine seats at the table were full and Connie marched in with a big smile and sat in the final empty seat.

"Okay, everyone. Welcome to needlepoint for beginners. This class will go for eight weeks and at the end we'll have several projects completed. And if you are interested after that, you can move on to the intermediate class. This class will give you a taste of the craft and see if it's a fit for you."

She looked around the table and had everyone introduce themselves and say if they'd ever tried needlepoint before. No one had. There was a range of ages, with Abby, Taylor and Beth being the youngest. Several people looked to be in their forties or fifties, and the rest seemed closer to Connie's age. Everyone seemed excited to be there.

Connie explained the basics of what they'd be doing, which was learning how to begin a project. They each took the materials they needed from the pile in the middle of the table. It was a little awkward at first and they all laughed as they fumbled with the needle and thread and tried to make even stitches.

Connie taught them all the different kinds of stitches and they practiced them all. By the end of the session, they had learned some of the basics and had a homework assignment to bring to the next class—a simple project that would use the stitches they'd learned.

"Take your time with it and don't worry if it doesn't look perfect. Just have fun, and we'll see you all next week. Take your materials with you—there are bags by the door for each of you."

They each grabbed a bag and put all of their materials in it.

"That was fun," Taylor said as they put their coats on to leave.

"It went by really quickly," Beth said. "Do you both still want to get some dessert? We could walk over to the counter at the pharmacy?" The Nantucket Pharmacy had an old-fashioned soda counter that served coffee, sandwiches, ice cream, and frappes.

"Yes, let's go." Abby led the way. It was a short walk to the pharmacy, and they slid onto three empty stools. There were only a few others there, so they had the place to themselves. Beth just got a coffee, Taylor got a coffee frappe and Abby ordered both a coffee and a dish of peppermint stick ice cream.

"So, Taylor, how are you liking the new job?" Beth asked.

"I'm loving it so far. Tomorrow I'm actually heading out to The Whitley Hotel. I'm tagging along with Victoria as she interviews a few people there, her wedding planner, Mia and Paula, the hotel's general manager. It's for a piece on over-the-top, extravagant weddings."

"That sounds fun," Beth said.

"We know Mia," Abby said. "She stayed at the inn for a while when there was a fire at her condo and we heard about some crazy weddings. She did Kate's wedding and our friend Angela's too."

"Angela's is a good example of an extravagant wedding," Beth said. "She married a famous author and film producer and they had over six hundred people there, on the beach."

Abby laughed. "They did one really smart thing too— the wedding favors were the director-style chairs. So all they had to do was have them delivered and set up and the guests all took their chair home."

"I love my chair. It's the one I always bring to the beach," Beth said.

"So Abby, how are you? I feel like we're always talking about me and my new job these days. What's new in your world?" Taylor asked.

Abby sighed. "Well, it hasn't been the best week, to be honest. Jeff and I have been trying, and I took a pregnancy test this morning. I was so sure that I was pregnant. But it was negative. It's just so discouraging."

"I'm so sorry." Taylor sounded so sympathetic that Abby felt her eyes fill up.

"Abby, I'm sorry, too. Are you thinking of trying the treatments again?" Beth asked.

"I really don't want to." She'd done the fertility treatments for her first pregnancy and it was such a roller coaster of emotions and hadn't worked. It wasn't until they gave up and decided to take a break from the treatments and trying that she suddenly found herself pregnant. The doctor said that was common and often the stress of trying got in the way for some people. "I was hoping it might be easier this time. I guess that was silly of me." She took a deep breath as a tear spilled over and ran down her cheek.

Taylor immediately handed her a paper napkin and Abby dabbed at her eyes with it. "I'm sorry. My emotions today have been all over the place. I almost cancelled on you guys, but Jeff talked me into going."

"I'm glad he did," Beth said. "We're here to support you. Let me know if there's anything I can do to help?"

"Me too," Taylor said. "And it's not silly of you. I

would have thought the same. Maybe it will happen again that way if you guys take a break and stop trying."

Abby sniffed and dabbed at her eyes again. She smiled. "That's what Jeff said, too. So, I guess that's what we'll do. Just try not to think about it for a while and see what happens."

CHAPTER 17

"How was the needlepoint class?" Blake asked Taylor the next morning. She and Victoria had just arrived and turned on their computers, and Blake stopped by their desks on his way to his office.

Victoria rolled her eyes. "Did you really take a needlepoint class? How did you get talked into that?"

Taylor laughed. "Yes. I went last night with two friends. It was actually fun. We're all beginners."

"My grandmother does needlepoint," Victoria said. The look on her face was priceless. The thought of willingly learning needlepoint clearly horrified her.

"Are you two heading out to The Whitley this morning?" Blake asked.

Victoria glanced at the time on her cell phone. "Yes. We should actually leave now. Are you ready, Taylor?"

"I'm ready." Taylor followed Victoria to her car, a white BMW hardtop convertible. "It's winterized,"

Victoria said as Taylor climbed into the passenger side. "It has all-wheel drive, which is good in the snow. Not that we get all that much of that here, thankfully." It was a gorgeous car.

Taylor wasn't surprised to find that Victoria was a fast driver. She zipped along and what should probably have been a twenty-minute drive to the other side of the island barely took fifteen minutes. When she pulled up to the front door of The Whitley Hotel, Taylor was impressed. It was a beautiful location right on the water. A sprawling building with small cottages on either side.

A valet came right over, and Victoria handed him her keys. They went inside and the lobby was even more breathtaking, with cool white marble everywhere and bright pink flowers in crystal cut vases throughout the room. A high cathedral ceiling with a glass roof let in lots of light.

A woman who'd been chatting at the concierge desk turned when they walked in and broke into a smile. She was holding an iPad and was dressed in a flattering navy pantsuit with a pale pink scoop-neck top. She walked over to Victoria and introduced herself to Taylor.

"Hi, I'm Mia Maxwell."

"Mia, this is Taylor. She just started at the paper and is going to sit in on our meeting."

"Great. Follow me. Paula is going to stop in for a few minutes too. She's the general manager and has worked here forever." She led them to a small conference room, and they sat around a long oval table. Taylor opened her notebook and got out her favorite pen, while Victoria opened her iPad and set out a mini-tape recorder. "I like to record all my interviews so I don't miss anything as long as that's okay with you?"

Mia nodded. "Of course. It's fine."

"Mia is doing my wedding and while it's not going to be as extravagant as the weddings we'll be writing about, it's still going to be amazing!" Victoria said proudly.

"Where are you having it?" Taylor asked.

"We haven't totally decided yet. The Whitley is one option. Todd also said he'd love to do an outside wedding at his parents' place, which is on the water. They have a big yard, so we could do a tent. That could be fun too, it's a hard decision."

"We still have lots of time," Mia assured her.

"So, Mia, tell us about your biggest, most over-the-top wedding that you've done so far?" Victoria asked.

Mia thought for a moment. "That was probably last summer, here at The Whitley. If you like, I can check with her and see if she'd allow mention of her name. She might like that, actually."

Victoria perked up. "Yes, if you wouldn't mind, that would be awesome."

"So, her family has a gorgeous estate here. I actually suggested they hold the wedding there as you said, with a big tent, and overlooking the water. It would have been stunning. But she had her heart set on The Whitley."

Victoria glanced at Taylor. "This is by far the nicest, most exclusive hotel on Nantucket."

Taylor nodded. What she'd seen of it so far was beautiful and she could only imagine how lovely it must be in the summer.

"So, the family was from the Upper East Side and money was no object. They wanted the best of everything and lots of it. She had a dozen bridesmaids and ushers. They chose very expensive wines and champagne and it was all open bar. They put all their friends and family up at the hotel and had a full weekend of activities, from brunches to cocktail hours and wine tastings. Some of them golfed while others shopped. The menu was over-the-top decadent." She listed off all the courses, including lobster and steak, and by the end of it, Taylor's mouth was watering.

There was a light knock on the door, and they all turned.

"Paula's here!" Mia introduced Paula Whitley, the general manager, to Taylor and Victoria.

"Mia was just telling me about one of her most extravagant weddings, which was held here," Victoria said. "Do you recall any others?"

Paula laughed. "Where do I start? I've worked here for years and there have been so many. We've had some celebrity weddings. Those are always fun and sometimes challenging. We once had a famous actress that wanted to have a live zebra at the wedding."

"A zebra? How would that even be possible?" Victoria asked what Taylor was thinking.

"It's not. Maybe in LA or New York City, but the logistics of getting a zebra to Nantucket are impossible. Even if it was possible, I don't think it's fair to the animal.

We convinced her instead to borrow an all-white horse and ride up to the beachside ceremony on horseback. It was dramatic enough that she went for it."

"I remember seeing pictures of that one," Mia said.

Paula told them several more stories of over-the-top weddings, which Taylor just couldn't relate to at all. Especially the expense which seemed so wasteful. But she also couldn't fathom having a million or so to blow on a wedding.

"I bet you have your share of difficult bride stories too?" Victoria asked.

Mia and Paula exchanged glances.

Mia chuckled. "Off the record, yes. But for obvious reasons, I don't want to be quoted complaining about any of my former clients. That's not good for business."

"Well, I don't mind sharing some general stories. I can't get too specific for the same reason as Mia. But we've had our share of diva brides. I think most of them are otherwise nice people, but the stress and emotions of the wedding sometimes push them over the edge."

Mia smiled. "That's being generous."

Paula laughed. "Let's see, there was the bride that asked us not to rent out half of the rooms so her party could have the hotel all to themselves. We told her we'd be happy to do that, but she'd have to pay for the rooms. She just didn't get it. She came around, though. They usually calm down once everything is all sorted out."

"Do you have any upcoming celebrity weddings?" Victoria asked. The question surprised Taylor as she imagined that something like that would be confidential.

"We generally have at least one a year, it seems. But one of the biggest challenges with a celebrity wedding is security. We handle all our celebrity weddings and guests in general with the utmost confidentiality. Typically only myself and one or two staff members will know there is a celebrity here."

Victoria grinned. "I figured as much, but I had to ask. We've actually heard there are a few celebrities on Nantucket right now for a Cami Carmichael project."

From what Taylor had read in the tabloids, she knew that Paula's brother Nick, the assistant chef, was also dating Cami Carmichael, so Paula likely knew if the rumor was true.

Paula just smiled. "Do you have any more questions that aren't about celebrities?"

"Sure. Any tips on how to throw a luxury wedding without breaking the bank?"

Paula thought about that for a moment. "Yes. You can keep things simple and still have a lovely, elegant wedding without going over-the-top. Focus on one thing that you really want and go all out for that. Maybe it's the food, or the location. It doesn't have to be everything. Sometimes the most memorable weddings are the ones where one element really shines."

Mia nodded in agreement. "I think that's so true."

Victoria turned off her recorder. "I think I have everything I need. Thank so much, both of you."

On the way back to the office, Victoria asked Taylor what she thought of the interview.

"It was interesting. I really appreciate you letting me

tag along." She found it fascinating how different Victoria's style was from Joe's. Joe really took the time to talk to his subjects first, to get to know them. Victoria talked about herself and then dove in rapid fire with questions. It was more about her than the interviewer. But she still ended up with what would likely be a fun story.

"So, Paula didn't confirm it, but by wanting to change the subject when I asked about Cami Carmichael, that tells me she is here and probably other celebrities too. Or she would have said otherwise."

"Right. Though we sort of knew that anyway from the tabloids," Taylor said.

"They lie though. I needed to confirm, and now that I know for sure that Cami Carmichael is here, I am on a mission to get an interview with her and anyone else famous that might be filming here."

"How do you plan to do that?" Taylor was genuinely curious.

Victoria laughed. "I'm not sure yet. But I am going to figure it out."

CHAPTER 18

"So, you'll never believe what I walked into this morning," Rhett began as Lisa handed him a glass of cabernet. They'd just settled at the kitchen island for dinner and were starting out with wine and some cheese and crackers while they waited for Lisa's meatloaf to be done.

"What happened? Something good, I hope?" Lisa cut a slice of cheddar and added it to a cracker.

"It's a good thing I went in early today. When I got there, I was faced with quite a sight. Someone had thrown a bucket of red paint on the front of the building and wrote the words 'This food sucks' on the door."

"What? Who would do that?"

"Well, the first people that came to mind were the Winkleton twins. After all, they're not happy that I decided to press charges."

"Do you really think they would do that, though?"

"Unfortunately, yes. And they're not the sharpest knives in the drawer. It apparently didn't occur to them that I would have a camera on the front door too."

Lisa laughed. "You got it on film?"

Rhett nodded. "Yes. It was early this morning, around six, and they didn't even bother to cover their faces. Really not smart of them."

"So, what did you do?"

"I called Dave down at the station and emailed the video clip over. This is not going to help their case when their court date comes up in a few weeks."

Lisa shook her head and took a sip of wine. "Were you able to get it cleaned up?"

"Yes, we just power washed it off. Not the way I wanted to start my day though."

"No. What do you think will happen to them? Will they actually go to jail?" Lisa asked.

Rhett had wondered the same thing. "I don't know. I think it's their first offense, so if they do go to jail, it won't be for long. It will go on their record though, and hopefully that will keep them out of the restaurant business. I'd hate to think of them doing this to someone else, and I'm pretty sure they would. They really had no remorse about it and no good reason to do it."

"Is there ever a good reason to steal?" Lisa asked.

"No, of course not. But some people really need the money—for whatever reason, they are desperate enough to steal. They just did it because they could. I found their entitled attitude disturbing."

Lisa reached out and squeezed his hand. "I'm glad you had a camera out front and that they are gone. Hopefully that's the last that you'll see of them."

"Right. On a happier note, I hired two good people today, to fill their roles. Solid referrals with good references. And I think we upgraded, as both are year-round people with lots of experience. Jose, the new guy I hired for the bar, has a following—the place he worked at last year was sold and he took time off and went down to the Florida Keys for the winter."

"Good. As my mother used to say, everything happens for a reason."

Rhett laughed. "And mine used to say what doesn't kill you makes you stronger."

Lisa smiled. "Seems like both apply. And I think that meatloaf is just about ready."

A few minutes later, Lisa handed him a plate with thick cut meatloaf smothered in mushroom gravy, mashed potatoes and green beans. It tasted as good, if not better, than anything he served in his restaurant.

"I could have hired you to replace Aidan," he teased. "Seriously though, this is great. Thank you."

"It did turn out pretty good, didn't it?" Lisa agreed.

Halfway through their dinner, an idea came to him.

"How would you feel about going off-island this weekend? Might be fun to spend a night or two at the Chatham Bars Inn and have a nice dinner somewhere downtown."

"The Chatham Bars Inn? I hear that's really lovely.

Similar to The Whitley. I've never had the chance to stay there before. I'd love to do that."

"Good, let's do it. I'll book us for this coming Friday night. We can take the early boat over and do some sightseeing around Chatham, maybe take a drive down to Provincetown for lunch at The Lobster Pot.

"I'll book us on the ferry," Lisa said.

"Perfect. It will be nice to get away, just the two of us. We haven't done anything like this for a long while."

"So, Abby and Kristen will be filling in for me this weekend. Rhett's taking me off-island until Sunday," Lisa said over breakfast Thursday morning. Taylor had just sat down with a loaded plate of cheesy grits with scrambled eggs and diced andouille sausage. Lisa was finishing a bowl of oatmeal, and Rhett was sipping on his usual black coffee.

"That sounds fun. A romantic getaway," Taylor said.

Lisa smiled. "Yes. I'm looking forward to it. Have you been to Chatham?"

"Once. A few years ago, I rented a place with friends in Truro for a week. We drove to Chatham one day and ended up having a great dinner at a small place off Main Street. I can't quite remember the name, something to do with an Oyster."

"The Impudent Oyster?" Rhett suggested.

"That was it! Have you been there?"

"No, but two other people recommended it too, so we might have to try it, if Lisa likes the sound of it."

"With that many recommendations, I'm in. I don't really care where we go. I'm just looking forward to having a little adventure. How are things going for you at the paper? Any interesting new stories?"

"Good. I actually went with Victoria the other day to The Whitley and listened in on an interview she did on over-the-top weddings. It was interesting and that hotel really is gorgeous."

"It's lovely. I'm curious to see how the Chatham Bars Inn compares," Lisa said.

"I can't wait to hear all about it."

"You know, I may have a story for you," Rhett said. He glanced at Lisa. She raised her eyebrows and then nodded. She obviously knew what he was referring to.

"So you know how those Winkleton twins stole money and food from the restaurant?"

Taylor nodded.

"Well, they apparently weren't happy with me and decided to get some revenge, with a can of red paint...." He started to tell Taylor what happened and after a few minutes she asked him to pause for a moment and ran to get her notepad and pen. He started from the top and walked her through everything that had happened—how he installed the security cameras and how the camera by the front door recorded everything.

Taylor didn't know if she'd be able to write the story, as Joe usually handled the crime beat, but she'd talk to him and Blake and at least pass on the information.

Taylor ran into Blake on the way into the office and told him about Rhett and the Winkleton twins. "I know it's Joe's beat, so I can give him all my notes."

"No, it's your story. Your source. You can run with it. Right, Joe?" Joe had walked in behind them and was sipping a large cup of coffee.

"What's that?" Joe asked.

"Taylor knows Rhett, who had an issue at his restaurant. Couple of brothers that stole from him and then vandalized it. You don't care if she runs with it?"

Joe shrugged. "Not at all. Go for it."

Taylor felt a thrill of excitement. It would be a fun story to put together.

"Good, that settles that, then. You're on for trivia tonight, I hope—both of you?"

"I'm in," Joe said and headed off to his desk.

"Me too. I'm looking forward to it," Taylor said.

"Good, as it looks like there's just the three of us able to go tonight. Mary and Emily can't make it."

The three of them, Joe, Blake and Taylor, headed over to the Rose and Crown after work and settled at a table near Owen, the trivia announcer. He was just getting his equipment set up when they arrived, and he came over to chat for a minute when he saw Blake and Joe. He nodded at Taylor. "I see you're back."

Blake smiled. "Owen, this is Taylor, she's recently started with us."

"Good, the more trivia recruits the better." He chatted with them for a few more minutes, then went back to his setup.

A waitress came over and they ordered a round of drinks while trying to figure out what they wanted for dinner. When the waitress returned with their cocktails, they were just about ready to order. Blake went with a bowl of chowder and the short rib taco appetizer. Taylor was about to order one of the salads but then saw someone walk by with the lobster mac and cheese and that settled it. Just as Joe was about to order, his phone buzzed and he looked concerned when he saw who it was.

"You guys, I have to take this. I'll be right back." He stood as he answered the phone and walked off for some privacy.

"I'll come back in a few minutes." Their waitress said before heading to another table.

Taylor reached for her wine and took a sip. Dreaming Tree Crush was a red blend that she hadn't tried before.

"Oh, this is really good." It was smooth and jammy, just delicious.

Blake laughed. "You sound so surprised."

"You never know with wine when you try a new one, especially when you're in a pub that only has a few options. This was a nice surprise."

"True. It's more of a beer place." Blake was drinking Cisco Wandering Haze, a local IPA.

Joe returned a moment later, looking a bit shaken.

"I'm so sorry, but I have to go. That was Dover Falls, the assisted living where my mother lives. She just took a pretty bad fall and they're taking her to Nantucket Hospital. I'm going there to meet them."

"Oh no. I'm so sorry, Joe," Taylor said.

"I'm sorry too. Keep us posted, Joe."

"Thanks, guys. Good luck, hope you crush it tonight."

Taylor watched Joe leave and her heart went out to him.

"That's a scary thing," she said.

Blake nodded. "His mother just moved in there recently. It's a wonderful place, and her dementia was getting so bad that she couldn't live alone anymore."

Their waitress returned a few minutes later. "Looks like it's going to be just the two of us," Blake told her.

"I'll go ahead and put your order in then."

"It's going to be harder with just the two of us," Taylor said. She suddenly felt a bit nervous. She'd been perfectly comfortable when it was the three of them, but now that it was just her and Blake, she didn't know if she was imagining it, but there seemed to be an energy shift. It felt sort of date-like to be sitting there having dinner, just the two of them. But she told herself that was ridiculous. And not likely to happen again on trivia night.

"It might be harder, but you never know," Blake said. "I've seen plenty of small teams of two and sometimes even one person do really well. Sometimes it's easier to agree on an answer. Of course, it really all depends how the questions fall and if one of us knows the answer."

She smiled. "Right. That makes sense."

"How's your story on Rhett's restaurant coming along?" he asked.

"I actually emailed it to you right before we left. I think it turned out okay. It was an interesting story. I wonder how often that kind of thing happens with restaurants?"

"Good. I'll look at it first thing tomorrow. As to how often, unfortunately, from what I hear from my restaurant friends, and I know quite a few people that work in the business, it's common. Especially what happened at the bar—that's easier to manipulate. Either by not ringing a sale up and just pocketing the cash, or ringing up a house brand on a premium pour and pocketing the difference."

"That's so awful. I can't imagine how stressful it must be to have employees outright stealing like that."

"It's a tough business. Lots of turnover and high expenses. Many restaurants don't make it past their first year. I think I'll stick to the news."

Taylor laughed. "Right. More fun to go to restaurants and support them that way."

"Cheers to that," Blake said.

"Did you always know you wanted to work at the paper?" Taylor asked. She was curious to know more about him.

"No. I worked there when I was a kid because it was convenient. But then once I was in college, I went for the jobs that my friends had, that were more social, like working as a lifeguard and then as a bartender. I think because the paper was always an option, I wanted to try other things."

"When did you realize you wanted to focus on journalism?"

"A few years after graduating. I had a liberal arts degree, and I really didn't know what I wanted to do. I bounced around trying a few different fields, mutual fund accounting, insurance sales, and advertising at a magazine. I didn't really love any of them, but at the magazine I kind of got bit by the writing and publishing bug. I wasn't great at advertising, but I liked editing ad copy and writing. And I missed Nantucket. So here I am."

"It took me a while, too. I actually don't know all that many people that are doing what they thought they'd be doing when they graduated college."

"How are you liking things so far at the paper? Is it what you expected?"

"Better actually. I'm glad to be here," Taylor said as their waitress returned with a basket of hot bread and butter. The restaurant was beginning to fill up, and she recognized a few familiar faces from the week before. Blake was easy to talk to and had her laughing with some of his stories from his early days at the paper.

"I wasn't exactly welcomed with open arms. There was some resentment from a few people that figured I'd be a spoiled brat. Fortunately, that didn't last long. I made mistakes, of course, but they could see I was taking it seriously and trying."

"What was it like working for your father? Did you learn a lot from him?"

He chuckled. "He was probably tougher on me than anyone else. But that's how I learned. He was one of the best. You'll meet him soon. He spends his mornings here once he's back on the island. And I still like to bounce things off him now and then."

"I look forward to it."

Their food arrived, and they shifted their focus to eating. The lobster mac and cheese was decadent—delicious but very rich and Taylor barely ate half. She wrapped up the rest to take home. Blake had no leftovers. They finished just as Owen came around with the trivia score sheets.

Once trivia started, they were mostly busy focusing on trying to come up with answers. They had absolutely no idea on some of them and just laughed as they tried to come up with something that had a chance.

"My dad will be back in time for Daffodil weekend. He rides his vintage Ford Model T every year. My mother and her friends will be waiting at the end in 'Sconset with their over-the-top tailgate."

"That sounds so fun. Will you go too?" Taylor asked.

"I think I might ride along with my dad. I usually do. It's a good time."

"Well, I'll look for you then and make sure I get a good snapshot. Since I'm covering the parade."

Blake laughed. "We'll see. Maybe you can get a good shot from a distance with lots of cars in it."

Taylor was surprised that going into the final question she and Blake were in third place.

"I've won before with just two people," Blake said. "Let's do this."

The final category was geography, which Taylor didn't feel good about. "I don't think I will be much help on that."

But Blake felt confident. "I usually do well with that category. Let's go big and bet it all." So they did. And when the final question was read, Blake groaned.

"I have no idea. I'm sorry." Blake scribbled an answer down and handed it to Owen. When the final answer was announced, they did not get it right.

"Oh well. Next week will be better," Taylor said.

Blake grinned. "Yep. Still always a fun night out though."

When the bill came, Taylor put out her credit card, assuming they'd split the bill, but Blake waved it away. "My treat this time." Taylor hesitated, feeling awkward. "I insist." He handed the check and his card to the waitress.

"Thank you."

Once he signed his charge slip, they headed out and walked back to the paper. It was a clear night, not too cold, and Taylor could smell the salt of the ocean as the wind blew past them. The short walk only took a few minutes.

"So what do you think about Nantucket so far? Could you see yourself staying here a while?" Blake asked. It was dark out, so she couldn't see his expression.

"Yeah, I think so. I know I haven't been here long, but it really feels like home. Maybe that sounds silly?"

"No, I don't think it does. I get it. I can't imagine living anywhere else," Blake said as they reached the building.

"Goodnight, Blake. See you in the morning."

CHAPTER 19

"We should really do this more often," Lisa said as she looked out the window of their room at the Chatham Bars Inn. The hotel was even nicer than she had imagined. The room was large and had a lovely view of the ocean and Lisa was impressed with the Nespresso machine, which was in the room instead of a regular coffee maker.

"I'm going to get one of these for the dining room at the inn. I bet guests will love having the option to make an espresso or cappuccino with their breakfast."

Rhett put his arms around her from behind and rested his chin on the top of her head. "I totally agree, about doing this more often, that is."

Lisa laughed. "But not about the Nespresso machine?"

"I'll still be drinking my black coffee, same as usual. But you're probably right."

Lisa turned around and wrapped her arms around his

neck, and he dipped forward for a sweet kiss. She was having the best time. They'd arrived the day before, checked in and spent the afternoon walking around Main Street in Chatham, doing some sightseeing and shopping before having a delicious dinner at the Impudent Oyster. Today the plan was to have breakfast downstairs in the hotel restaurant and then hit the road and drive to Wellfleet and play a round of golf at a course that overlooked the ocean.

Rhett had done his research and found that the Highlands course was good for beginners, which was Lisa's level. They'd brought all of their equipment with them. Once they got on the road, it didn't take long to get there, maybe a half hour or so as the traffic was light this time of year. It was cool, so they dressed warmly, but the sun was shining and there was little wind, so it wasn't too cold. The view from the course was gorgeous. It was high on a hill overlooking the ocean.

When they finished playing, they drove on to Provincetown at the very tip of Cape Cod. Commercial street was quiet this time of year, but it was still fun to see all the different shops, art galleries and restaurants. They had lunch at The Lobster Pot, which was right on the ocean and had so many lobster dishes it was hard to decide. But they both settled on baked stuffed lobsters with a traditional Cape Cod Ritz cracker stuffing and they ate every crumb.

By the time they got back to the hotel, it was late afternoon. After such a big lunch, neither of them were hungry, so they decided to rest up, and then head out to catch a movie and have popcorn for their dinner and maybe a drink after at the Chatham Squire downtown and maybe catch some live music.

But by the time the movie finished up, it was nearly nine, and they were both tired after running around all day. They decided to head back to the hotel and have a drink at the pub there, which was cozy with polished dark wood. Lisa was surprised by how quickly the weekend went and they both said more than once that they needed to do it again soon.

CHAPTER 20

Monday afternoon, Taylor was deep into edits on a story and enjoying the peace and quiet in the newsroom as she had it all to herself. Both Joe and Victoria were out in the field doing interviews. She was just about to hit send to email her latest story to Blake when Victoria whooshed into the room on a cloud of excitement and dropped her tote bag on her desk so loudly that Taylor was startled and looked up.

Victoria was all smiles. "I got it! I found where Cami Carmichael is filming and got a bunch of pictures. Wesley Stevens is in the cast!"

"Wesley Stevens? Really? Wow." He was a major star. And gorgeous. He was in his mid-thirties and had been nominated for an Oscar for his last film. Taylor hadn't heard anything about him being on the island.

"I know, right? I don't think anyone knows he's here yet. This a huge, major scoop." Victoria turned on her computer and uploaded the pictures from her phone.

"Check this out…" She turned the monitor so Taylor could see.

"That's a great shot." It was a closeup of Wesley and he had a very photogenic face. "Did he let you take that?" Taylor had always heard that he valued his privacy and it was rare to see photos of him online.

Victoria laughed. "No. I didn't ask. He doesn't have a reputation for being cooperative."

"Oh. So how did you get the shot then?"

"I took it from behind a tree. Look, I got a great one of Cami too."

Taylor looked at the next picture on the screen. Cami had her arms around Wesley's neck and her eyes were half-closed. They looked about to kiss. Victoria clicked to the next picture, which was of them with their lips locked. "Isn't this awesome? They make a great-looking couple."

Taylor frowned. "They're not a couple, though. I thought she was dating Paula's brother?"

Victoria shrugged. "She might be. But you have to admit, these two look great together."

"Were they filming a scene, though? They're not really together."

"I think they were filming, yes. But the chemistry is intense. People will think they're a couple when they see these pictures."

That's what Taylor was afraid of. She thought of how much trouble Victoria's pictures had caused Marley.

"Are you sure you should run them? They make it look like there's something there that isn't actually happening. At least say they are just filming."

Victoria thought about it for a moment, then grinned. "I suppose I could do that. I don't want to get into trouble again."

"Did you try to talk to them?"

"I did, yeah. I walked over and asked if I could interview them and they practically ran away from me. The answer was a resounding no. They really didn't look happy to see me."

It didn't sit right with Taylor that now Victoria was going to publish pictures that Cami and Wesley didn't even know she'd taken.

"I don't think they're going to be happy about this," Taylor said.

Victoria shrugged again. "Probably not. But that's part of the business. It's what they signed up for when they became celebrities."

Taylor wondered if anyone really willingly signed up to be a media target. A quick google search showed that there wasn't anything illegal about it, unfortunately as it came down to expectation of privacy and as Victoria had said, celebrities didn't have that the same way that a normal citizen would. It still felt wrong. She wondered what Blake's opinion on it would be.

"ARE YOU SURE YOU DON'T MIND ME GOING TO MIA'S tonight? Since I was just out Tuesday night for the class?" Mia had invited her to a Pampered Chef party and usually Abby hated those kinds of things, unless they were

Pampered Chef. The food was always good. She liked the few things she'd bought before and she could use another cookie sheet. Plus, her sisters were going as well as Paula, her sister Lucy and cousin Hallie from The Whitley, too, so it should be a fun group.

Jeff scooped up Natalie from where she was sitting on the sofa, flipping the pages of her favorite Elmo book. He gave her a hug and a kiss. "Of course I don't mind. Natty and I have some reading to do. And I know it won't be a late night, right?"

She laughed. "No, it starts at six and I'm sure I'll be home by nine."

"So go and have fun. Remember, that's the doctor's orders, to relax." Abby had met with her doctor earlier in the week and they'd discussed starting up infertility treatments again but decided to wait a few months so that Abby could de-stress about it all. The doctor had suggested meditation and yoga, both of which had seemed kind of out there to Abby, but she'd agreed to try.

And much to her surprise, she was enjoying both, especially the meditation. She'd found a few guided meditations on YouTube and found that they calmed her nerves well. And the same with yoga. She was a beginner at it, so she started with some gentle easy classes, also online, and found she was sleeping better and overall feeling more relaxed.

"Okay, I'm off then. I'll see you in a bit."

Abby grabbed the bottle of wine she'd picked up earlier. Mia had said she was taking care of snacks, but if people wanted to bring something to drink, that was fine. She'd picked up a bottle of Bread and Butter chardonnay, which she knew just about everyone liked.

Mia lived with her sister Izzy in one of the condos by the wharf. Abby arrived right on time and saw that her sisters, Kate and Kristen, were already there.

"Come on in and help yourself to a glass of wine. There's a bottle of red and white already opened," Mia said as she took the bottle of wine from Abby. "Thank you for this. I'll put it in the fridge for now."

Abby poured herself a glass of chardonnay and smiled when she saw that it was the same as the one she'd brought. She took her glass over to where her sisters were sitting on a long sofa, while a cute little white dog, a Pomeranian, lay at their feet.

"That's Penny," Mia said. "She's friendly and social. Loves having lots of attention." Abby sat and automatically reached down to scratch Penny behind her ears.

"Kristen is going to have Mia do her wedding," Kate said.

"You are?" Abby was surprised. She didn't see Kristen as wanting a big wedding and thought if you used a wedding coordinator, it was usually for something bigger.

Kristen nodded. "I honestly have no interest in managing all the details. That's not my strength. It won't be a big one, but it will be nice to have someone else do the legwork. Tyler actually suggested it. He knew I was dreading getting started with it all."

"I was the same way, if you remember?" Kate said.

Abby laughed. "That's true. Maybe it has something

to do with both of you being creative. That's great though. I'm sure she will do an awesome job. Any idea where you might want to have it?"

"We are thinking maybe late summer and possibly a clambake on the beach. Neither one of us wants anything too formal."

"A summer clambake sounds perfect," Abby said.

Everyone else arrived a few minutes later, helped themselves to wine, and settled on the chairs Mia had set up in the living room.

There was a woman talking to Paula that looked familiar, but Abby wasn't sure who she was. Until she laughed and Abby immediately recognized her smile. "You guys, is that Cami Carmichael?" She whispered to her sisters.

Kate nodded. "I think her real name is Bella."

Once everyone was seated, Mia looked around the room. "I think everyone knows just about everyone, except maybe Bella. Bella, this is everyone." She introduced everyone by name, and Bella nodded. "Nice to meet you all."

"Bella almost didn't come," Paula said. "Because of what just happened with the local paper. But I told her she didn't need to worry about anyone here."

"What happened?" Abby asked. "I haven't seen the paper."

"A reporter snapped some pictures of Bella and her co-star that made it look like there was something romantic going on," Paula said. "That kind of thing makes me so mad!"

Bella smiled. "Especially when I'm engaged to Paula's brother. Nick understood. He knew it was just shots from the show we're filming. But the reporter didn't make it very clear. It's just frustrating. Wesley was furious. I get why he hates the media."

They all agreed that it just wasn't right.

Bella sighed. "I know it goes along with what I do. I just wish I had a little more control over it."

The subject changed and the party consultant began her presentation, showing them the various kitchen products and had them sample some fun appetizers that could be made using the cookware. While Abby was nibbling a veggie and cream cheese stuffed croissant, a thought came to her. Bella was seated just two people to her left.

"Have you thought about proactively doing an interview with the local paper and telling them what you want them to know? To get ahead of any speculation?" She asked.

Bella looked dubious. "It crossed my mind, but I'm sure it's a small paper and I don't think I could bring myself to ask for an interview with the reporter that snapped those pictures. She asked us while she was there and we said no. We had no idea she'd already been busy with her camera."

Abby assumed that was Taylor's co-worker, Victoria. "One of my best friends is a reporter there, and she's not the one that you met. There are two of them, well three if you count Joe, but he's been there forever and doesn't handle these kinds of stories. Taylor is a sweetheart, and you'd be in safe hands talking with her."

"That's a possibility. I'll think about it," Bella said.

"I'll let her know. She's going to be covering the Daffodil Festival this weekend. If you are going, you could talk to her then—or another time." Abby realized Bella might not want to attend such a crowded event.

Bella looked thoughtful. "Nick mentioned that to me. Paula and Lucy are having a big picnic, and Nick is going to do all the food. It does sound fun." She grinned. Maybe if I wear one of my disguises, I can do it—I have a black wig and dark sunglasses and as long as I don't smile much, I'm usually safe."

"Our family will be there too," Abby said. "My mother and her friends have a big picnic planned. It really is a fun time. People go visiting from picnic to picnic."

"Okay, tell your friend if I go, I'll pop down to your picnic and if she has time, we can chat a bit. Maybe I'll let her get a picture of me and Nick together, actually."

Abby loved the sound of that. She knew Taylor would be thrilled and maybe a little freaked out, too. "Great. I'll let Taylor know."

CHAPTER 21

"Are you serious? Cami Carmichael might actually talk to me?" Taylor had just settled at her desk Friday morning when Abby called.

"It's not definite. And her name is actually Bella. She said that if she decides to do it, she'll come find our picnic at the Daffodil Festival. After you take all your pictures, you have to join us. My mother goes all out—all of her friends bring food. It's a lot of fun."

"Okay. I'll plan on that and I won't mention anything to anyone yet, just in case it doesn't happen."

Victoria walked in on the tail end of the conversation and raised her eyebrows when Taylor ended the call. "What aren't you mentioning? Do you have some good gossip?"

Taylor laughed nervously. Victoria was the last person she'd confide this news to. She wouldn't put it past her to show up at the parade and try to push her way into an interview.

"Oh, nothing. A friend just told me I have to join her family's picnic at the parade this weekend. I've never been before."

"She's right. If someone invites you to their picnic, you don't want to miss out. It's a good time. I'll be there with Todd's family. Their personal chef is grilling filets topped with béarnaise and buttered lobster tails. The Veuve Clicquot will be flowing too."

Taylor shook her head. "That sounds incredible and unlike any picnic I've ever been to."

Victoria laughed. "It's completely over-the-top. People try to out-do each other. But it's a lot of fun too. You're covering it for a story, right?"

Taylor nodded. "I am."

"Well, that will be a good one for you." Victoria's phone rang, and she turned around to take the call.

Taylor checked her email and settled in to start her day, but her attention was distracted by the possibility of an interview with Cami Carmichael. It would be so huge if it happened.

———————

IT DIDN'T TAKE TAYLOR LONG TO GET LOST IN HER WORK, and before she knew it, the day had flown. Somehow, it was already four when Blake walked through the room with a big smile. "Let's all call it a day and go for a round of after-work drinks, on me at the B-Ack Yard BBQ. Who's in?"

"I'm just about done with this story. I'll call Todd and

have him meet us over there when he gets off," Victoria said.

"I'm in. Let's go." Joe stood, turned off his computer, and grabbed his jacket.

Blake glanced at Taylor.

"I'm ready, too."

Fifteen minutes later, just about the whole company was at B-Ack Yard BBQ, sipping cocktails at the bar. Everyone was excited about the parade the next day.

"My grandchildren are coming over in the morning from Yarmouth. They look forward to this every year," Mary said.

"My mother said she's going all out. She and her friends have quite a feast planned. My father and I will be eating well when we get to the finish line," Blake said.

"It's like a football tailgate, but way fancier," Joe added.

"I'm really looking forward to it," Taylor said. "My friend Abby invited me to her family's picnic. It sounds like her mother is cooking up a storm for it."

"She owns the inn you're staying at, right?" Blake asked.

Taylor nodded. "She does. I'm only there for a few more weeks. It's been great, but I'm eager to get settled in my cottage."

"Do you need any help to move?"

Taylor thought it was nice of Blake to ask, but she couldn't help laughing a bit too.

"I have all of one big suitcase, so I think I can

manage. The cottage is furnished, so I didn't bring much. It will be fun getting anything else that I need."

Blake nodded. "My dad flies in tonight. You'll meet him tomorrow and you'll start seeing him around the newsroom. He's an early riser, so he usually comes first thing and leaves at lunchtime."

"Does he do any writing?" Taylor was curious about his father, wondering what he did as part-time chairman.

"When he feels like it he writes a bit. Usually opinion pieces. And he analyzes all of our numbers and then tells me where I'm going wrong." Blake laughed. "And he's usually right."

Taylor and Blake both turned as Victoria's phone started pinging.

"Is someone texting you?" Mary asked after the fifth ping in rapid succession.

Victoria glanced at her phone and started thumbing through the messages. She looked excited.

"These are notifications about those images I took. Looks like they got picked up by the AP." She grinned. "Guess who just went viral again?"

"Your pictures of Cami Carmichael?" Taylor asked.

"Yes, and Wesley Stevens."

"Nice job, Victoria. Cheers to going viral," Blake looked pleased.

"Thank you!" Victoria waved at her fiancé Todd as he walked in and ran over to share her good news.

Taylor still had mixed feelings about those pictures. When the others were engaged in conversation, so that they wouldn't overhear, she softly asked Blake, "Does the paper often run pictures like that—ones that were taken without the person knowing?"

Blake frowned. "They didn't know she took them?" He seemed surprised.

Taylor had assumed that he knew. "They didn't want to be interviewed," she said.

He stayed quiet for a long moment. "It is disappointing that they wouldn't do an interview. But that's their right. I don't encourage this kind of thing, but Victoria was also within her rights to take the pictures. They were out in public and they are celebrities. They don't have the same expectation of privacy that you or I would."

Taylor nodded. "I know. It just doesn't feel right to me. Especially as some people will assume there's a relationship there because of the photos."

Blake looked confused. "She did state that they were pictures taken on a film set. So there shouldn't be any confusion."

"She did. But they are talented actors and have good chemistry. People will wonder."

Blake took a sip of his beer. "We can't control what people think."

"No, I don't suppose we can."

"Victoria's a hustler. She's out there finding stories. It's not a bad thing." He smiled. "You're doing a great job, too. Your story on the twins that robbed Rhett's restaurant was a good one."

"Thank you." He'd told her it was good when she handed it in too and he didn't want as many corrections, so Taylor was encouraged. It was nice to hear it again, though.

"Blake Ojala! It's been way too long. How are you?" Taylor turned to see a tall, beautiful woman with shoulder-length blonde hair and icy blue eyes walk over to Blake and give him a big hug. She was impossibly thin, and wore a sleeveless top that showed off sleek, toned and tanned arms.

"Andi! Did you move back here? It's been a long time." Blake looked happy to see her.

She nodded. "I just flew in from Naples last night. I'm going to be working from here remotely this summer. Although my father has talked about moving the business here year-round. I'm not sure he means it though—Naples is a lot warmer than Nantucket in the winter."

"You're still working with his company?"

"Yes, still crunching numbers. Business is good." She glanced over at a table where three people were being seated. "I should go join my friends for dinner. Just wanted to say a quick hello. I'm sure I'll see you around."

"Definitely. Are you going to the parade tomorrow? Dad and I are riding in it."

She laughed.

"Yes, I'll be there. I'll keep an eye out for you."

She walked off and Blake was still smiling as he turned his attention back to the bar and his employees. Both Mary and Taylor had watched the exchange with interest.

"Potential girlfriend?" Mary asked.

Blake chuckled. "I'm sorry I didn't introduce you

both. That was Andi, an old friend. We dated a little, a long time ago. I don't think I see it happening again."

Taylor wasn't so sure. There was definitely some chemistry there.

Mary seemed to agree. "Never say never...." She said.

CHAPTER 22

Saturday morning breakfast was quiet when Taylor arrived. Usually Abby, Kate and Kristen stopped by to visit with their mother, but they'd all be seeing her shortly at the parade. The inn was full of guests, though. Every room was booked and the dining room was busy. Taylor helped herself to a slice of spinach and artichoke quiche and a few pieces of cantaloupe and joined Rhett and Lisa.

They were saying goodbye to another couple that was heading out to the beach for a walk after eating. Taylor sat and sipped her coffee before diving into the quiche. Rhett, as usual, was just drinking coffee, while Lisa looked like she'd just finished eating a bowl of cereal.

"Are you excited about the parade?" Lisa asked. "You've never been here for the Daffodil Festival, have you?"

"No. Abby told me all about it though and I am actually covering it for the paper, so I'm looking forward to it. Abby said you made a lot of food."

Lisa smiled. "I did bake up a storm yesterday. I made a few lobster quiches, a cheese board with some fun new cheeses I haven't tried yet, a lemon and sun-dried tomato hummus, and some stuffed mushrooms. I think Paige is bringing a Caesar salad, and Sue is making cheesy garlic bread. Marley said she'd bring a dessert. Oh, and Chase is bringing a grill, and some marinated steak tips. He said we needed some red meat."

Rhett nodded. "I would agree with that."

"Can I bring anything?" Taylor asked.

Lisa shook her head. "No. Just yourself. The girls are bringing either Prosecco or champagne, so we will have plenty of everything."

Taylor was tempted to mention that she might also have an interview with Cami Carmichael, thanks to Abby, but she didn't want to jinx anything, as it wasn't definite. She was hopeful, though.

AFTER SHE ATE, TAYLOR WENT FOR A WALK ON THE beach, then showered, changed and headed over to Abby's. They were going to ride to the parade together. Jeff and his brother were going to meet them there later. So, it was just Abby, Taylor and Natalie that headed into town to catch the beginning of the parade.

All the cars were lined up, and many were decorated with daffodils.

"They're all so gorgeous!" Taylor was surprised by how well-kept the old cars were.

Abby laughed. "These are their babies. The guys that own these cars are true collectors and they love to show them off."

Taylor walked along, snapping pictures of the different cars. She kept an eye out for Blake and his father, but there were over seventy-five cars in the parade. Eventually, though, she saw them. Or rather, Blake saw her first and his waving arms caught her attention. He and his father were sitting in a bright red Ford Model T with creamy white leather seats. Taylor waved back and was about to walk over to say hello when Abby said they needed to leave.

"We have to hurry, so we don't get stuck behind the parade. We'll go find everyone and watch from our picnic spot. Then we can see them all as they drive by."

"Perfect, I should be able to get some great shots that way." Taylor followed Abby and Natalie back to the car and they headed off to Siasconset on the other side of the island which is where the parade finished and where everyone set up their picnic spots along the side of the road.

When they arrived, Abby's brother Chase was there with his wife Beth. Chase was setting up the grill. Lisa, Rhett, and her friends Sue, Paige and Marley were there along with their husbands and boyfriends. Kate, Jack and the twins arrived a moment after they did, and Natalie ran over to her younger cousins. The only ones missing were Kristen and Tyler.

"They're always late," Abby said. "They should be along any minute."

It was still early, just a little past eleven thirty, so Taylor wasn't hungry yet, but she happily accepted a mimosa when Lisa offered one. It was mostly bubbly Prosecco with a splash of orange juice, and it was delicious.

"It will still be a bit before the parade makes it out here. But we have plenty of food to keep us busy until then," Abby said as she cut herself a slice of cheese from the tray that her mother had just set out on a table that was filling up fast with food.

"Have a mushroom while they're still warm," Lisa encouraged as she uncovered a tray of stuffed mushrooms. Taylor reached for one, took a bite, and sighed. It was stuffed with a mixture of finely chopped sausage, spinach, onion, breadcrumbs, spices, and topped with parmesan cheese.

Abby laughed when she saw Taylor's expression. "Pass me one of those, will you? They usually disappear first."

"I can keep an eye on Natalie if the two of you want to walk around," Kate offered. "It might be good for Taylor's story to see the variety of picnics here."

"That's a great idea. I'll gladly take you up on it. Come on Taylor."

Taylor set down her mimosa, so she'd have both hands free to take pictures, and followed Abby. They walked a good way down and then crossed over and walked back on the opposite side of the road. Taylor had thought they might be exaggerating a bit about the extravagant picnics, but if anything, they understated it. Most of the picnics were lavish parties, many with private chefs manning the grill and gourmet food being served. Lobster and steak were common menu items.

And some of the appetizers were quite fancy too, everything from hand carved sushi to caviar, foie gras, fried chicken strips and scallops wrapped in bacon. It all looked great, and Taylor found herself starting to feel hungry again. They ran in to Victoria on their way back and sure enough, she was with her boyfriend's family and their chef was plating up buttered lobster tails as they walked by.

"You can get a picture of us if you want," Victoria suggested. She pulled her boyfriend Todd over and they posed by the chef as he poured béarnaise sauce over perfectly grilled steaks. They were all drinking champagne. The picture came out cute and seemed to capture the feel of the event.

When they returned to Lisa's spot, Kristen and Tyler were just arriving and Chase was putting steak tips on the grill. Taylor looked around for her mimosa and saw that her glass looked fuller than she remembered.

"I just made a new batch and topped that off for you," Lisa said.

"Oh, thank you!" Taylor sipped her mimosa and nibbled on the many snacks while she people-watched. There were still so many people arriving and setting up their picnic blankets and settling in to watch the parade.

She'd been looking as they walked around, but hadn't seen any signs of Bella yet. And then she stopped looking as Chase handed out steak tips and they loaded up their plates with steak, lobster quiche, garlic bread and Caesar salad.

They sat Indian-style on one of several big blankets. They were lucky as it was a relatively warm day for mid-April and the sun was shining.

"This is such a fun tradition," Taylor said as she looked around. Everyone was happily eating, talking, and laughing.

"It really is. We've been coming for as long as I can remember and I look forward to it every year," Abby said.

They ate their fill and relaxed and chatted for another hour or so before the parade reached them.

"The cars!" Natalie jumped up excitedly and went to run toward the edge of the blanket, but Abby grabbed her and pulled her close. "Stay here, honey. We can see all the cars just fine from here."

Sure enough, the first of the daffodil-covered vintage cars slowly made its way toward them. Taylor stood to get a better look and got her camera ready. She actually had a real camera now instead of just her cell phone. It was one of the first things she'd bought when she arrived on Nantucket and she'd got the best one that she could afford.

She took hundreds of pictures, snapping away as the cars cruised by, honking their horns, and everyone waving as they passed. Blake and his father were laughing as they drove by, and Taylor thought they looked quite a bit alike. His father was older, of course, with thick white hair and a good tan. They both looked like they were having a great time. Taylor got some good pictures of them before Blake spotted her, nudged his father, and they both waved.

Just as the last car passed, Abby called her name. Taylor turned and saw that she was talking to a tall, handsome man and a petite woman about their age with shoulder length black hair, dark sunglasses and a pink Red Sox hat. Taylor walked over to them and Abby made the introductions.

"Taylor, this is Cami Carmichael, I mean Bella, and her fiancé, Nick Whitley."

"Oh, it's so nice to meet you both. Bella, I didn't recognize you with that hair."

Bella laughed, and then Taylor instantly recognized her smile.

"It's amazing, isn't it? When I first met Nick, I was staying at the hotel and wore this wig everywhere and as long as I didn't smile, no one looked at me twice."

Nick laughed too. "I had no idea. Not even after we'd been dating a while. I guess that means I should get out more, maybe?"

Bella playfully swatted his arm. "Very funny." She turned back to Taylor and looked more serious. "Abby said you might be willing to do a story that shows how things really are with me, and with Nick?"

Taylor nodded. "Yes. I would love to."

"How about I get you both a mimosa?" Abby offered.

"I'd love one and I know Nick would too. Thank you." Abby went off to get their drinks while Taylor led them to a quiet spot away from everyone. They sat and Taylor got out her notepad.

"Do you mind if I record our conversation, too? I want to make sure I don't miss anything."

Bella and Nick exchanged glances before Bella nodded. "That's fine."

Abby returned a minute later and handed them each a mimosa, then left to go check on Natalie.

"So, what would you like to share? I'm sure people would love to know more about the project you're filming here?"

Bella smiled. "I'm happy to talk about that. It's a project I'm really excited about, for Netflix. It's an ensemble mini-series based on a book that I fell in love with. It has strong women and spans several generations. And our cast is phenomenal. We got very lucky. Everyone I wanted was available and excited about the story, too. It doesn't usually happen like this."

"I saw that Wesley Stevens is one of the main actors?"

"Yes, and he's been a dream to work with. He's a brilliantly talented actor."

"Why film on Nantucket?" Taylor was curious about that.

Taylor grinned. "I'd film everything here if I could. This is home now. It's where I met Nick." She gave his hand a squeeze. "I met him when I stayed at The Whitley for a few months. Nick is the assistant chef there. Truthfully, I think I fell in love with his food first."

Nick laughed. "She liked the way I cooked her salmon."

"I did! But then we fell in love too and this is where Nick is from and where he works. So, now it's my home too. Eventually, of course, I'll have to travel to shoot at other locations, but as often as possible I'll push for projects to be done here."

"Will you get married at The Whitley, then?" The beautiful hotel seemed tailor-made for a celebrity wedding like theirs.

"We haven't decided that yet. It's possible. If it was just up to me, I might want to go to town hall and not make a fuss. But, we know that's not fair to our families."

"They'd kill me," Nick confirmed. "I'm the first in my family to get married, and my mother is definitely more excited about the actual wedding part of it than we are. I just want to be married."

Bella glanced at him and the love they shared was so sweet to see. After a moment, she turned her attention back to Taylor.

"So, we might do something in between, maybe get married on the beach in front of the hotel. We need to consider security too, and if word gets out to the media. No offense, but it can be an issue."

Taylor immediately felt like apologizing for Victoria. "I understand that. I'm assuming you'll keep it as quiet as possible."

"Yes, we want to make sure it doesn't get too crazy." Taylor felt for them. She couldn't imagine what it must be like to be a target like that. Even though she was technically part of the media, she didn't support the behavior that many of her colleagues considered fine.

Bella looked all around, and Taylor wasn't sure what she was looking for until she leaned in and spoke softly. "It looks like no one is looking our way right now. If I yank off my wig, do you want to quickly shoot a few pics of me and Nick?"

"Oh! Yes, of course." Taylor got her camera ready and as soon as the hat, wig and glasses came off, she started snapping pictures. Bella and Nick side-by-side with their arms around each other, gazing into each other's eyes, laughing and smiling—that unmistakable smile. She took as many pictures as she could and hoped that some of them would be good.

After just a few minutes, Bella was done and pulled her wig back on, then her hat and sunglasses, and suddenly she was unrecognizable again. She laughed at Taylor's expression.

"I'd suggest you take a few of me in my disguise, but then that would defeat the purpose of it."

Taylor laughed too. "Right. I was just marveling at the fast transformation."

Bella and Nick were easy to talk to, and the interview had felt more like a conversation.

"We should probably head back," Nick said as they all stood up.

"Nick's family has a big picnic further down. This is my first time coming to the Daffodil parade. He told me it was a big deal, but I had no idea."

"It's my first time, too. It's hard to really imagine until you see it. Now I get what all the fuss is about," Taylor said. They walked over to Abby so Bella and Nick could say goodbye.

"This should be in the paper in a few days," Taylor said.

"Great, I look forward to it," Bella said as she and Nick turned to leave.

Once they were out of earshot, Abby turned to her. "So, how did it go?"

"Better than I'd hoped. Thanks again for suggesting it."

"No problem. Did you get any good shots?"

Taylor scrolled through her pictures. She got quite a few good ones of the cars, and a cute one of Blake and his father. When she got to the ones of Bella and Nick, she felt a thrill. She handed the camera to Abby to take a look.

"Taylor, these are awesome of Bella and Nick. I can't wait to read your article. This is huge for you."

Taylor realized that it really could be. If her story got picked up by the national media, it might go viral and it would be a great one to get out there with her name on it. She had a good feeling about it.

"There you are!" Taylor looked up and saw Blake walking toward them. She introduced him to Abby.

"Are you having fun?" he asked.

"Yes, this is incredible. So fun."

He smiled. "Had a feeling you'd like it. Everyone does. Did you get some good shots? Talk to anyone interesting?"

"I did. I actually interviewed Cami Carmichael and her fiancé, Nick Whitley."

He looked so surprised that she almost laughed.

"No kidding? How did you manage that?"

"Well, it was thanks to Abby. She met her recently and suggested it."

Blake nodded at Abby. "Thank you for that." He glanced back at Taylor. "Can't wait to read it. Want to take a walk? I'd love to introduce you to my father, and mother too."

"Sure. I think we'll still be here for a while?" Taylor asked Abby.

"Yes, go ahead. No one is in a hurry to leave," Abby assured her.

"We're not that far down," Blake said as they started walking.

"Was it fun riding in the car?"

Blake smiled. "It was, and it made my dad happy, so I'm glad for that. His flight was delayed, so he didn't get in til late last night. He was worried he might miss it."

"Is he starting back at the paper soon?" Taylor was curious to see what it would be like to work with his father.

"He's planning on being there bright and early Monday morning. I told him not to expect me there that early. He's usually the first one in."

"I look forward to meeting him."

"Well, here we are." They hadn't had to walk far at all to reach his parents' spot. There were a dozen or so people gathered around a folding table that held food and drinks. They did not have a personal chef, but Blake's father was manning the grill and flipping burgers as they walked up.

"Dad, this is Taylor, our newest employee," Blake introduced her.

His father smiled, wiped his hand on a napkin, then held it out to greet her.

"Nice to meet you. Blake tells me you're covering the parade. Hope you got a good shot of us."

"I did! It's a gorgeous car."

He looked pleased to hear it. "Thank you. I've had Betsy for over twenty years. Take her for a spin now and then to keep the motor going."

Blake's mother walked over and Taylor recognized her immediately. She had chin length blondish white hair that was in a crisp bob and she had the same eyes as Blake. "Mom, I'd like you to meet Taylor, from the paper."

His mother stared at Taylor, trying to place her. "Taylor. I know you from somewhere else, don't I?"

Taylor nodded. "I think we're in the same needlepoint class."

"That's it!"

"I didn't know you were taking that class," Blake sounded surprised.

"I don't tell you everything, dear."

Blake's father started taking burgers off the grill and putting them on a platter. "Would you like a burger?" he asked.

"No, thank you. We just ate. There was so much food."

Blake chuckled. "There always is."

"Victoria is here too. Did you see her?" She asked.

He nodded. "I ran in to her on the way to find you. Her group has quite the spread."

"And a personal chef," Taylor added.

"Not surprising. For a lot of people it's a competition and Victoria likes to win."

"What do you do at the paper?" His mother asked.

"I'm a reporter." It felt kind of funny saying that because it was still so new, but she liked the way it sounded.

"Taylor's doing a great job—and she just did an interview you're going to want to read," Blake said.

His mother raised her eyebrows. "Really? Who is it?"

"She got an exclusive interview with Cami Carmichael, here at the parade."

His mother looked all around. "She was here?"

"She was. She was in disguise, with a black wig, so she wouldn't be recognized," Taylor said.

His mother looked skeptical. "I think I would have recognized her if I'd seen her."

Taylor laughed. "She walked right up to me and I didn't recognize her at all until she smiled."

"She's famous for that smile. I've seen all of her movies," his mother said.

"Mom loves romantic comedies," Blake added.

They chatted a while longer until Taylor grew a little nervous about the time. She didn't want to keep Abby waiting if she and Natalie wanted to leave. "I should probably head back. I'm not sure what time Abby was planning to stay until."

"People usually aren't in a hurry to leave, so you should be fine. I'll walk back with you though."

Taylor said goodbye to his parents. "I'll see you Monday morning, Taylor," his father said as they left.

"That's funny that my mother is in your needlepoint class. It's not her usual thing."

"I had no idea either. No one uses last names there. I just know her as Ginny. She goes with her best friend Edith."

He nodded. "That explains it. Edith must have talked her into it. Normally Edith would have been here today, but she's out of town this weekend." He laughed. "So, is my mother any good at needlepoint?"

Taylor smiled. "As good as the rest of us. It's actually pretty easy."

They walked along silently for a moment, and then Blake surprised her.

"Do you have any plans this coming Saturday?"

"No, other than moving into my cottage that morning. Why?"

"There's an event at my parents' country club, a book talk with a local author, Philippe Gaston. He's had some bestsellers and films made of his books. It might be interesting for you and you could cover it for the paper. I'm going as I'm a big fan of his stuff, but if you're interested, you could come with me. Especially now that you specialize in interviewing celebrities."

Taylor didn't hesitate. "I would love that. I'm a huge fan of his books too."

They were just about back at the Hodges' spot. Chase was putting the grill away, and Abby was buttoning Natalie's sweater. The air was growing cooler, and it looked like people were getting ready to leave.

"All right, it's settled then. Plan on next Saturday night, and I'll see you Monday morning."

CHAPTER 23

"It's a good problem to have, Lisa." Marley and Mark were sitting around the island in Lisa's kitchen Sunday night. Lisa had invited them over for a last-minute grilled fish dinner after Rhett and Mark caught several big bass that afternoon. Rhett had just brought the tray of grilled fish inside and it was resting on the stovetop while they enjoyed a cocktail and some cheese and crackers and salted Marcona almonds.

"I told her the same thing," Rhett chimed in. "The way I see it, we have two options, either expand the kitchen again, or outsource to a bigger commercial kitchen."

"If you do that, outsource it. You won't have to handle as much of the baking and shipping yourself. It's not a bad way to go," Marley said.

"And you could have them do a set amount, so you always have some ready to ship," Rhett added. "That could take the pressure off from what you are doing now."

Lisa nodded. "Maybe I will look into that. I don't think I want to expand the kitchen again. That will only mean more work here for me and more people I'd need to hire. I don't think I want that here."

Marley smiled. "I'm not at all surprised to hear it, though. I told you those lobster quiches would sell well. Especially through sites like Goldbelly, which has really taken off."

Lisa added a splash of wine to her glass and topped off Marley's and Mark's as well. "I found it hard to believe when you said that. I'm just astounded by how sales keep increasing from month to month. And I've even cut back on the advertising because we didn't want to get overwhelmed."

"Now you are getting a lot of repeat business and word of mouth is really the best advertising," Marley said.

"I suppose so. I'm grateful, just surprised." Lisa cut herself a slice of cheese and looked contemplative as she added a cracker and popped it in her mouth. A moment later she spoke, "I don't suppose there are any commercial kitchens like that on Nantucket?"

Marley wasn't sure about it, either. "I really don't know. What do you think, Rhett?"

"I can ask around, but I kind of doubt it. We might need to go off-island."

Lisa frowned. "How would that work, though? Doesn't it have to be somewhere nearby, so I can go there?"

"You'd only have to go for an initial meeting or two, to share your recipe and do some quality control to make sure it bakes up the same," Marley explained. "Once that's set, all you'd need to do is tell them how many you want baked and where to ship to. You'd probably have to have them ship weekly to a distributor that will fulfill the orders that come in."

Lisa looked unsure. "That all sounds very complicated."

"Once, it's all set up, it should be much easier for you to manage everything," Rhett said.

"Well, that would be wonderful. This has ended up taking a lot more of my time than I ever anticipated," Lisa admitted. "Not that I'm complaining, I'm not. I thought it was a fluke at first, but sales are remarkably steady and growing."

"Do you let your guests know that you have the quiches available for sale?" Marley asked. "I bet quite a few might want to order too, especially around the holidays."

Lisa laughed. "No. Would you believe I've never mentioned it to any of them? I mean, it is on the website, but I could also leave a note about it in their rooms, and email them."

"It's always easiest to sell to people that already know and like you—and if they've tried your quiches, they should be good prospects," Marley said.

"There are so many things to think of. That's a great suggestion though." Lisa turned to Mark. "How is your online store going? I know Marley helped you with that a while back."

"It's going well. Not the volume you are seeing, but I'm happy. I'm reaching new people and past clients are placing orders too. It's amazing how the internet has opened up these kinds of possibilities." He glanced at Marley and squeezed her hand. "The best part, though, was meeting Marley."

He leaned over and gave her a quick kiss. Ever since their dinner when Mark apologized and then told her he loved her, and she said it back, they'd been spending even more time together and things were going better than ever.

"It was," Marley agreed. She then turned her attention back to Lisa and Rhett. "So, tell us all about your Chatham trip. I know you mentioned at the parade that you guys had fun, but I'd love to hear more specifics. Mark and I were thinking about going off-island soon and maybe that's where we'll head."

Lisa's face lit up. "Oh, you should. We had a great time. First, we stayed at the best place and that restaurant that was recommended, was so good." She went on to tell them all about the hotel and other places they went, and Marley paid close attention. Mark had said they could go wherever she liked, and from what Lisa said, Chatham seemed like it could be a great option.

TAYLOR JUMPED AT THE SOUND OF FOOTSTEPS BEHIND HER.

She'd thought she was the first one in the office Monday morning when she went in a little earlier than usual to work on her story and get it to Blake as soon as possible. She turned at the sound and then smiled as she saw the thick head of white hair and realized it was Blake's father walking toward her. They were at the entrance of the kitchen.

"Good morning, young lady. How are you this fine Monday morning?" His eyes were twinkling and he seemed to be in a wonderful mood.

"I'm good. Thank you."

He looked at her for a moment before saying, "Tracy right?"

"Taylor actually."

"That's right! I'm sorry. Taylor it is. I'm just heading in for a fresh cup of coffee. Would you like one? I made a big pot."

"Sure, I'd love some."

Taylor followed him into the kitchen and took the mug of coffee that he poured for her.

"Busy day ahead?" He asked.

"Yes. I came in a little early to write up the parade story."

"Oh, that's right. Did you get some good pictures, too?"

She smiled. "I did. Quite a few actually."

"Good. Well, I look forward to seeing your article when it comes out." He looked around the empty newsroom. It would still be a good half hour or so before anyone else came in.

"I really do miss this place in the winter. I've spent many happy years here. And now Blake will continue the tradition." He took a sip of his coffee. "Well, I have a column to write, so I'm off. Have a good day."

"You too."

Taylor got to work on her story and about an hour after Blake arrived she finished and emailed it to him. She got up to stretch her legs and went for a fresh cup of coffee. On her way back to her desk she ran into Blake and his father walking down the hall towards her. She smiled at both of them

"Blake, I just emailed the parade story to you."

He looked pleased to hear it. "Great, I'll take a look at it shortly."

"If you have any story ideas, let us know. I'm sure Blake has told you that already? It's always fun to see Nantucket through a new person's eyes," His father said.

"I haven't encouraged that yet, actually. But you're right of course. Taylor if you come across anything that seems like it would make a good story, we'd welcome it."

TAYLOR WAS SURPRISED BY HOW MUCH SHE WAS ACTUALLY enjoying the Tuesday night needlepoint class. It was easier to do than she'd expected and her Christmas ornament, an angel, was coming along nicely.

They all chatted as they worked on their projects in the group. Everyone admired each other's work and

Blake's mother smiled and said hello when she arrived and saw Taylor.

"When does your article come out in the paper?" Abby asked once they were all settled around the table.

"It should be out tomorrow." Taylor was admittedly excited to see it in the paper and hoped that it would be well-received. Blake had told her she'd done a good job, and he only wanted a few minor corrections made. Victoria didn't know anything about it. Taylor hadn't mentioned it and was actually a little nervous about her reaction once it hit—and especially if it went viral.

She got the impression that Victoria was still hoping she'd get someone on the set to agree to an interview, so she might not be happy when she saw that Bella had agreed to talk to Taylor. But maybe Taylor was worrying about nothing and Victoria wouldn't care. She hoped that was the case.

"I can't wait to read it," Beth added.

"Thanks. Did you and Chase get the house you put the offer in on?" Beth had told them at the parade that she and Chase were waiting to hear on an offer for a house they hoped to fix up and flip.

"We did! We just heard last night. There were five strong offers, but ours was a cash offer and we waived the inspection. That's one advantage of having a husband in construction—he inspected it when we looked at it."

"Congrats!" Abby said. "Will you need to do much work to it?"

"It looks really run down from the outside and the inside had the most hideous wallpaper you've ever seen, but it's just minor cosmetic stuff. Fresh paint and a few tweaks to the kitchen and bathrooms should be all it needs." Beth sounded excited, and Taylor was intrigued.

"Abby said you and Chase have done a few of these projects before. It sounds fascinating."

"It really is. It's a lot of fun to fix them up and then flip them. Chase handles the renovation work and I do most of the design stuff, picking out the colors and tiles and helping to market them."

"Would you and Chase be interested in being interviewed? I could do a profile on his business but also talk about how you do the flips. That might be really interesting for readers."

"I'll talk to Chase about it. If it was up to me, I'd say yes, though. I'll talk to him tonight and let you know tomorrow."

In a lull in their conversation, Taylor overheard Blake's mother talking to her friend Edith.

"I think I've finally found a good candidate for Blake. She stopped by our picnic at the parade and she's a beautiful girl, from a good family. Andi Richards, her father Tom, runs Richards Financial Group and Andi works with him. I don't know what she does, but I do know they work with high net worth clients and they do very well."

"Tom Richards. Isn't his wife, Muriel, on the Nantucket Arts committee?"

"Yes, and that is one of the biggest charity events of the summer. She and Blake dated a little, years ago. I thought I noticed a spark-at least on her end. Blake might need a little push."

"He needs to get back out there," Edith agreed.

"He will. If I have any say about it. I've been suggesting that he ask her to some book thing he said he wanted to go to at the country club. He said she mentioned it to him and is already going, so that sounds promising."

Taylor didn't like the sound of that. She wondered if it was the same book talk he'd invited her to? Not that she supposed it mattered, as it wasn't like it was a date, it was just a work thing. Though she was excited to go to the country club with Blake. To get dressed up and maybe for just a second or two pretend that it was an actual date. She reminded herself, though, that it wasn't a good idea to have feelings like that about her boss. She was pretty sure dating one's boss was a terrible idea—assuming he was even interested. And she had no reason to think that he was.

THE NEXT DAY STARTED OUT UNEVENTFULLY. TAYLOR HAD breakfast as usual with Lisa and Rhett, then headed into the office, greeted Blake's father, who was pouring coffee when she arrived. She chatted with him for a few minutes, then brought a fresh mug of steaming black coffee to her desk and got busy.

The first thing she did was look up her article. It was in the paper, as expected, and it gave her a thrill to see that they'd put it on the front page, both her coverage of the parade and her interview with Bella and Nick. She'd expected a reaction of some sort from Victoria when she arrived, but she didn't give the paper a glance and hopped right on the phone to do an interview, then scheduled another and ran out the door soon after. Taylor guessed that since Victoria didn't have any featured articles in this edition that she couldn't be bothered to see what else was in it.

Which suited Taylor just fine. She had plenty to do, beginning with some research for an interview later in the week. The rest of her day flew by and it was business as usual until around three in the afternoon when suddenly her inbox blew up with notifications that her article was being shared. The AP wire service picked it up, along with many of the online celebrity tabloids, and a quick search of social media showed that people were sharing it all over Facebook and Instagram.

Blake came out of his office a few minutes later and high-fived her just as Victoria walked in the door. His father was right behind him. "Nice job, Taylor. You're getting a ton of shares, especially on the Bella interview. How does it feel to go viral?"

She grinned. "I like it!"

His father nodded. "Good job young lady."

Victoria frowned. "What are you talking about? Who is Bella?"

"Cami Carmichael," Blake said. "Her real name is Bella."

"Taylor interviewed her?" She looked right at Taylor. "How did you get her to agree to that? She totally shot me down."

"She knows my friend Abby, and she wanted to set the record straight and introduce her fiancé Nick—so no one would think she and Wesley were an item."

"I would have been happy to talk to her about that!"

"I don't think she was too keen on you, since you took those pictures of her," Blake reminded her.

"Oh, well. I suppose so." Victoria flopped into her chair, turned her back to them, and focused on her computer screen. Taylor could feel the annoyance coming off her in waves. Victoria clearly felt that Taylor had stepped on her toes by doing that interview. She felt bad and glanced at Blake. He just shrugged.

"You win some, you lose some. You did a great job, Taylor. Keep it up." He and his father went back to their offices. Taylor turned her attention to her computer. Twenty minutes went by before Victoria turned around and her tone was a bit friendlier.

"So, what was she like?"

"Bella? I mean Cami Carmichael. She was really nice. Normal. You'd never know she was a huge movie star. She and her boyfriend are down to earth."

"Does she live here now? I heard rumors about that," Victoria asked.

Taylor nodded. "She said she considers Nantucket home now. She and Nick are engaged, and he's from here and works at The Whitley."

"That's cool. So, what else are you working on?" Victoria hadn't paid any attention to what Taylor was doing before.

"Nothing that exciting. I have a meeting with the

Whaling Museum at the end of this week. I'm doing a piece on the history of the museum and the current whaling industry. What about you?"

"I'd still like to track down her co-star, Wesley Stevens. I haven't given up on that story. Did she mention anything about him?"

"Just that he's great to work with. And that he hates the media."

Victoria made a face. "I'll get him to come around."

CHAPTER 24

"It's been lovely having you here, Taylor. I'll miss seeing you at breakfast," Lisa said as Taylor joined her and Rhett early Saturday morning on her last day at the inn. Taylor had been thinking the same thing. She was going to miss the morning chats and Lisa's delicious food.

"I'll miss it too," she admitted. "It's really been wonderful staying here."

"I'm sure you're excited to get settled into your new place, though," Lisa said.

"I am. I've only seen pictures online, but it looks really cute. I don't think I'm going to have to do too much, as it's furnished. I'll just go grocery shopping and pick up whatever else I need."

"Well, maybe Abby will bring you by some Saturday when the girls come for breakfast. I'm sure we'll find a way to keep in touch," Lisa said. "They should actually be here any minute."

"I'd love that. Did you make any decisions about outsourcing your baking?" Lisa had told her that she needed to expand and was looking into some options.

"Yes! Rhett found a place just outside of Boston that will work with me. They will bake the quiches and then send them to a distributor that will handle the packing and shipping. It's a little scary to let go of it, but I think it might be a good thing."

"It will," Rhett assured her.

"That's exciting. And it should free up some time for you too?" Taylor knew that Lisa was spending most of her days lately baking and at times, it was overwhelming.

"I hope so. We'll still do plenty of baking here too, but hopefully it will be a more manageable schedule this way."

Taylor took a sip of coffee, then smiled as she saw Abby and her sisters walk into the dining room. Natalie was with her and ran immediately to give Lisa a big hug. Kate had the twins with her as well. She set them down in their carriers. Both were still asleep, so she took advantage of the few quiet minutes to join Kristen and Abby to get a coffee and some food. Once she was back at the table, both babies were stirring, so she set up their playpen and moved them both in it along with their blankets, and favorite toys.

"So, are you ready for the big move today? Are you sure you don't need any help?" Abby asked.

"Thanks. I'm sure. I don't have that much stuff with me."

"I can't wait to come see it."

Taylor smiled. "I'll have you all over soon. I can't wait."

"What are you girls all up to tonight? Any fun plans?" Lisa asked.

"We're just staying in. I don't remember the last time Jack and I actually had a date night," Kate said.

"Well, you know you can always leave the kids with me if you guys want to have a night out. I've told you that before," Lisa reminded her.

Kate nodded. "I know. I didn't want to bother you, but I think we just might take you up on that soon. I've been asking around for babysitters but there's no one I really feel comfortable leaving them both with."

"Well, let me know. It will be good for you both to have a break and maybe get a nice dinner or something," Lisa said.

"I'll talk to Jack. Thank you."

"We're staying in tonight, too," Kristen said. "Tyler is going to cook. I think he's picking up some steaks. Oh, and I talked to Mia yesterday, and she's all set now to plan the wedding. So, that's a relief."

"Good. You'll love working with her. Have you decided on a date?" Kate asked.

"We're thinking early October, when the weather is still nice, but the crowds are gone. We still need to decide on a place. Mia is going to gather some options to show us." Kristen looked happy instead of stressed. Taylor could see the benefit of using a wedding planner. Although she kind of thought it would be fun to coordinate everything, but she knew it just stressed some people out.

"A few of Jeff's friends are coming over for dinner tonight. It's a kind of last-minute thing. Taylor, if you don't have plans, I'd love to have you join us. I think one of his friends might be single," Abby said.

"Oh, that sounds fun. I actually have plans tonight, though. I'm going to a book talk at the Nantucket Country Club with my boss, Blake."

Abby raised her eyebrows. "Is that a date?"

Taylor shook her head. "No. It's actually a work thing. He thought I could interview the author."

"Hmm. Interesting though that you're both going."

"Well, he was going anyway and had an extra ticket and suggested the interview."

"He is single, though," Abby said. "And a few years older than you. Easy on the eyes, too."

"I thought he was engaged?" Kate asked.

"He was. They were going to be married at The Whitley in December but broke up a month before," Taylor said.

"See, single!" Abby smiled.

Lisa looked concerned. "Yes, but he's her boss. That might not be a great idea."

Taylor agreed, unfortunately. "It's really not a date. I'm too new there to even consider that. I don't think it would be smart."

"Probably not," Abby agreed. "Too bad, though."

"I wouldn't necessarily rule it out," Kristen said,

surprising everyone. "You just never know where you might find love. Sometimes it works."

Taylor smiled, thinking of Connie Day, who had said something similar.

As tempting as the idea was, she didn't even know if Blake saw her as anything other than an employee. So, it was definitely safer not to even think that way.

"You guys, it's really just a work thing."

"Well, have fun. And call me tomorrow," Abby said.

CHAPTER 25

By the time Taylor said goodbye to everyone and headed back to her room, it was a few minutes past ten. She'd stayed and visited with Abby and her sisters and as they were all leaving, she gave both Lisa and Rhett goodbye hugs, too.

Now all she had to do was finish packing, which was mostly done except for a few stray items in the bathroom. Once everything was stashed in her suitcase, she zipped it up, grabbed her purse and her other big duffel bag, and made her way downstairs. She loaded everything in her car, checked the address on her phone, and plugged it into her car's GPS.

And exactly eight minutes later she pulled up to the small cottage with its pretty white picket fence. It was too early in the season for the pink roses, but she knew they'd be there by summer. There was a blue pickup truck in the driveway. Mr. Rugby, the landlord, had said he'd meet her there to give her the key and show her around the house.

Taylor grabbed her luggage and headed to the side door. Mr. Rugby climbed out of his truck and met her there.

"You must be Taylor. Rich Rugby." He looked to be in his mid-sixties and Taylor knew from their brief phone conversation that he was a native Nantucketer.

"Yes, nice to meet you."

"Here you go." He handed Taylor a set of keys, and she unlocked the side door and stepped inside. She went to grab her suitcase, but Mr. Rugby picked it up.

"I've got this." He followed her inside and set her suitcase by the wall. She dropped her other bags next to it and looked around. There were two rooms downstairs, a cozy kitchen and a roomy living room with a small fireplace and two sand-colored sofas, one full size and a smaller one, both facing the fireplace and television. The walls were a pale grayish blue.

"We redid this kitchen a year ago, so it has all new appliances and a disposal too," Mr. Rugby said proudly. It was an adorable kitchen, with all white cabinets and a light gray subway tile backsplash as well as an island that was too small to eat at, but added some workspace.

"It's perfect."

Mr. Rugby smiled. "Your bedroom and a full bath are upstairs. There's a half bath on this level and washer and dryer. There's also an outdoor shower and a small deck out back with a Weber grill. Trash pickup is once a week on Monday. If you have any issues with plumbing or heating or anything, just give me a holler. I don't expect you will, but you never know."

"Thank you."

Mr. Rugby looked around the room. "This was the first house that I lived in as an adult. When I got married, we lived here until we had our first child and then we needed more room. I've rented it out ever since. Have a few other cottages I've collected over the years and I rent those out, too. I'm retired now, so it keeps me busy enough."

"I love the kitchen. And this place has plenty of room for me." Taylor was excited to settle in.

"All right, then. I'll leave you to it. You know how to reach me if you need anything."

As soon as he left, Taylor dragged her suitcase upstairs and sighed happily as she caught a glimpse of the view out the bedroom window. The room wasn't huge, but it was all she needed and it had big windows with distant views of the ocean. A small desk sat in front of one of the windows. So if she wanted to, she could work there with her laptop and have an ocean view. There was also a full bathroom with a big soaking tub. Taylor mostly took showers, but the oversized tub beckoned to her. Maybe she'd pick up some candles and bath soap at the grocery store and try it out later that afternoon.

She spent the next hour or so unpacking and putting everything away in the chest of drawers by her bed and closet. Once just about everything was stashed away, she went downstairs and took a closer look at the kitchen. There was a Keurig coffee maker and in one of the cabinets someone had left an unopened box of lemon green tea. Taylor opened it and made herself a cup and thought about what she needed to get at the grocery store. The tea was the only thing in the kitchen, so she made a list of everything she needed, condiments, spices, and everything else she wanted to stock her cupboards and refrigerator with.

She spent the rest of the day shopping and getting her cottage organized. By late afternoon, she was ready for a break and took a long soak in the tub before getting ready to head out to the book event with Blake. It was at seven, and Blake hadn't mentioned anything about food, so Taylor made herself a small turkey sandwich for dinner. She wasn't sure how formal the event would be and debated what to wear. It was cool out and windy, so she decided to dress warmly and went with black dress pants and a pretty boatneck, cream-colored sweater and black boots with a bit of a heel. At only five three, she liked to wear heels occasionally.

At six-thirty sharp, there was a knock at her front door. Blake had arrived to pick her up. She ran a brush through her hair one final time, then went to greet him, opening the door wide. Blake stepped inside and looked around. Taylor had tried her best to add her own touch to the cottage, with some vanilla candles on the coffee table and island and a vase of fresh flowers on the kitchen counter.

"This place is great. Looks like you're all settled in?"

"Just about. I've been unpacking and shopping most of the day. Want the grand tour?"

Blake laughed. "Sure, show me around."

Taylor led him upstairs, and he walked over to the

window that faced the ocean. She noticed that he was dressed nicer than she'd ever seen before, with a navy blazer, light blue tie and white button-down shirt.

"Great view."

"It's distant, but I love it. There's an outdoor shower too. I've never had one of those before."

"They're common here—nice when you come home all sandy from the beach. You can rinse off outside."

They headed back downstairs, and Blake walked toward the door. "Are you all set to go?"

Taylor grabbed her coat and purse. "I'm ready." She followed Blake to his car, a gray Jeep Wrangler, and climbed in the passenger side.

Ten minutes later, they arrived at the country club and Blake led the way into a function room where there were at least a hundred people sipping cocktails and nibbling on both hot and cold appetizers. There was a bar in the corner and servers roamed the room with appetizers on silver platters. Taylor was glad she'd eaten lightly because everything she saw looked delicious. She glanced around and was relieved to see that there was no sign of Andi. Maybe she decided not to come to the event after all.

Blake saw her looking around and smiled. "The food is good here. What would you like to drink?"

"A chardonnay, please."

Blake walked off to get their drinks as a server came by and offered diced tuna with avocado on a puffy wonton chip. Taylor took one and savored it while she waited for Blake to return. She didn't have to wait long.

He handed her a glass of wine a moment later, and they walked over to a table that had cheese and crackers and sliced salami.

Taylor had just reached for a salami slice when a tall, dark-haired man walked over and said hello to Blake.

"Philippe! Good to see you. Meet Taylor. She's new to the island and to the paper. I thought if you had time, she might do an interview with you," Blake said.

Philippe smiled and held out his hand. "Great to meet you. I'm always up for an interview. Tonight might be tough, though. How about early next week? Tuesday morning is good for me if that works for you, around nine?"

Taylor nodded. Her schedule was wide open. "I can do that."

"We can meet in my office." He told her his address, and she recognized the street as being right on the ocean. She was starting to learn her way around.

Someone waved at Philippe and he excused himself. "I think I'm being summoned. Time to start the talk."

"Let's sit." Blake led the way to the front row of seats, where they'd have a good view of Philippe. Once everyone realized he was getting ready to speak, the seats filled up.

His talk was fascinating. Taylor had read several of Philippe's books as she loved a good mystery or suspense and his books were huge bestsellers that were a bit of both. She'd seen his most recent movie that was based on one of the books, too. He spoke about how he got started writing and the inspiration for some of his books. Then he read a short passage from his newest release and took questions from the audience.

After the talk, Philippe signed books and a local bookseller manned a table selling them. Taylor and Blake both bought a copy and waited in line to get it signed. When they reached him, Philippe smiled as Taylor handed him her book. He signed it with a thick black sharpie then said, "See you on Tuesday."

"Is Angela here?" Blake asked as he handed Philippe his copy to sign.

"No, she had plans with her girlfriends tonight. She'll be there Tuesday, though, when you come by, Taylor. Maybe you can mention her cleaning business too." He smiled proudly. "She started it from scratch and it's growing like crazy."

Taylor glanced at Blake. She wasn't sure if she could mention that or not. But Blake just nodded. "It's all good."

"I look forward to meeting her," Taylor said as they moved out of the way to let the next person get their book signed.

"Blake? I thought that was you. Are you a fan of Philippe's books too?"

Taylor looked up and saw Andi, smiling at Blake and looking as beautiful as ever with her blonde hair sleek and shiny. She was holding a stack of books, all written by Philippe. Another woman about her age, was by her side.

Blake smiled. "Hey. My mother mentioned you might be here, too. Yes, I'm a friend, and a fan of Philippe's stuff." He glanced at her pile of books. "But maybe not as big a fan as you. Did you get all those signed?"

She nodded. "I did. Have you met my sister, Kelly? She's a big fan too. We usually pass his books back and forth."

"Nice to meet you. This is Taylor, she works with me, and is going to do an interview soon with Philippe."

Andi glanced her way and Taylor could see the question in her eyes, wondering if there was anything more between her and Blake. "That's great," she said. "I look forward to reading it. We're heading off to meet some friends. Nice seeing you both."

They left, and Blake glanced at his watch. They'd been there for a little over an hour, but it was still early.

"Are you in a hurry to get home? We could get a drink here at the bar and maybe have dessert? It is Saturday night after all." Blake's eyes twinkled as he made the suggestion. And Taylor wasn't ready to go home yet.

"It is pretty early. That sounds good to me."

He led the way to the long, polished wood bar in the country club's main restaurant. There were a few others sipping cocktails and eating at the bar, as well as at the tables throughout the dining room.

They sat, and the bartender came right over and recognized Blake.

"Nice to see you, Blake. Are you here for dinner or just drinks?"

"Drinks, I think, and maybe some dessert. We just came from the book function."

"Quite a crowd for that." He handed them dessert

menus and took their drinks order. Blake got a Jack and Coke and Taylor switched to a glass of cabernet. A flourless chocolate cake caught her eye on the dessert menu, and she loved the combination of red wine and chocolate.

"Anything look good? I've had their chocolate cake, it's excellent."

"That's what I was looking at. I don't know if I'm hungry enough for a whole piece, though. Do you want to share? Or do you want your own?"

Blake chuckled. "I actually have a weakness for dessert. I was thinking about getting the apple pie. Get the cake, though. I'll still help you with it if you can't finish."

They put their orders in and five minutes later, their desserts were set in front of them. Taylor's was served warm, with a drizzle of raspberry sauce and a scoop of vanilla ice cream. It was decadent and delicious. Thankfully, Blake was true to his word and inhaled his apple pie and then helped her finish hers.

Taylor was amused that he had such a sweet tooth. She never would have guessed it. He ate healthy and was pretty active. He rode a bike that he kept tied up outside the office as often as he drove.

She sipped her wine and watched him polish off the remaining bites of her dessert. The more time she spent with Blake, the more she liked him. And the more she found herself attracted to him. She caught a whiff of his cologne as he leaned in for a final bite and his scent mingled with the rich chocolate was intoxicating.

She took another sip of wine and forced her mind to

go in a different direction. She shouldn't be thinking about him that way. He'd given her no reason to think he was interested in anything more than friendship, and he was her boss. Even if he were to show interest, she knew it would be a bad idea to act on a mutual attraction. She told herself it was just that he was the only guy she'd been spending any real time with. She needed to meet more people—people that she didn't report to.

"So, what do you think?" Blake was looking at her expectantly, and she'd completely missed his question.

"I'm sorry. I was in a sugar coma for a minute. What do I think about what?"

"I asked if you like to cook and if you do what you'd want to see in your kitchen if you could add anything? I'm going to be doing some renovating and totally redoing my kitchen. But I need some ideas."

"Oh! Well, I don't cook much, as it's just me. But I like to play around in the kitchen. Do you have an island? Are there any ocean views from your unit?" She guessed that there might be because it wasn't a long walk to the wharf from his office.

"There are some decent views of the harbor from my unit. I was actually thinking of totally shaking things up and moving the kitchen and living room upstairs and the bedrooms a level below. That way I could enjoy the views more. And there's no island now. You think I should have one?"

Taylor nodded. "Definitely, and I'd have it facing the ocean and have the stove top on the island, so you can enjoy the view while you cook. And have a few stools along one side so you can chat with people, too. And subway tile for your backsplash. And white cabinets. Maybe white on top and blue gray below the counter tops. That contrast might be cool. That's what I'd do, anyway."

Blake laughed. "You've thought about this before. I like the ideas, though. I hadn't thought about putting a stovetop on the island. Maybe I should have you come take a look and see the space—in case you have any other ideas."

"I'd love to see it." She'd been curious about what his unit looked like above the newsroom. She'd pictured it as fairly small, but hearing that it was actually two levels meant it was bigger than she'd thought. She knew the upside-down layout where the living area was on the top floor was fairly common on Nantucket and any ocean area, so people could have better water views. It seemed like a fun idea.

"Do you know who will do the renovations?" She asked.

"I haven't decided yet. I was going to ask around and get some recommendations. I don't suppose you know anyone?"

"Not personally, no. But Abby's brother Chase does that. He and his wife Beth run a construction company and Beth was telling me they do a lot of remodeling for clients and for their own flips."

"That's right. I should have thought of him. I'll make sure he's one of the people I talk to."

"Is your dad glad to be back at the paper?" So far,

every morning, Blake's father was the first person there.

"He loves it, yeah. I think he likes being part of the energy there and keeping his pulse on the business. I think he also likes getting away from my mother for half the day." Blake laughed.

That reminded Taylor of what his mother had said at the last needlepoint class. "I overheard a conversation at class the other night that your mother had with her friend Edith. She has plans for you," she teased.

"Oh no," he groaned. "Do I want to know what they are?"

"She approves of your friend, Andi. Has high hopes."

His expression was hard to read. "She always liked Andi. She knew I was thinking of going to Philippe's talk and she suggested I invite Andi." He smiled. "I told her my other ticket was already spoken for."

His smile was warm, and he held her gaze just long enough that those thoughts she'd tried to push away came rushing back. She looked away and reached for her wine. It was almost gone. She took the last sip.

"Would you like another glass?" Blake offered.

She shook her head. "No, I'm totally full. Thank you. This was fun. I'm looking forward to interviewing Philippe on Tuesday."

Blake pulled his credit card out and set it on the counter. The bartender came right over and took it away and returned a moment later with the charge slip. He signed it and stood. "Ready to head out?"

The ride back to Taylor's place was quick and quiet. She was sleepy from the dessert and the wine and guessed

Blake was likely feeling the same. He pulled into her driveway, and she was surprised when he turned the motor off and got out of the truck.

"It's dark. I'll walk you to your door." He was right. It was very dark, with just a sliver of moon in the sky and a sprinkling of stars. The temperature had dropped, and Taylor shivered as they walked to her door. She fumbled with her keys to find the right one and was glad she'd turned on the outside light. It was small, but she would have had a hard time with her keys otherwise.

"Thanks again for tonight and for the dessert and wine."

It was just light enough that Taylor could see Blake's smile.

"It was a good time. Thanks for keeping me company. See you on Monday."

CHAPTER 26

Marley finished whipping the mashed potatoes and checked the time. It was a quarter to six. Mark would be over in fifteen minutes. He was always on time. It was Sunday night, and she'd invited him to dinner as he'd taken her out both Friday and Saturday nights. So, she wanted to treat him to a nice home-cooked meal. She was making Lisa's short ribs, and they were simmering in the oven. When she opened the oven to slide the dish of mashed potatoes in to keep warm, the scent of the ribs made her mouth water. Hopefully, they would taste as good as they smelled.

She cut up some romaine lettuce and tossed it with a homemade Caesar dressing. It was actually Frank's recipe, but she knew it by heart—and it was easy, just a mix of good mayo, garlic, Worcestershire, lemon and a few spices. She tossed it with the lettuce in a big wooden bowl and set it on the kitchen island. The asparagus were also roasting in the oven. Everything was done now.

She poured herself a glass of the same wine she'd used for the ribs, a fruity zinfandel. She got one out for Mark too and filled it halfway. A moment later, there was a knock at the front door.

Through the frosted pane window on her front door, she could see Mark waiting. She felt a rush of warmth, happiness to see him, as she opened the door and welcomed him in. He stepped inside and a blast of cool air followed him. It was unusually cold for late April. She was still adjusting somewhat to the Nantucket weather. In California, where she'd lived for over thirty years, it would be so much warmer.

But she was very glad to be where she was, with Mark. He took off his coat, and she handed him the glass of wine.

"Something smells fantastic. What are we having?"

"Short ribs. Lisa's recipe. I hope mine turns out as well."

Mark leaned over and gave her a kiss. "I'm sure they will."

They nibbled on some salted nuts and sipped their wine while they chatted for a bit before Marley served dinner. Lisa's recipe turned out as good as she'd hoped and Mark went back for seconds on everything. When they were done and the dishes were cleaned up and leftovers put away, Marley topped off their glasses and they moved into the living room and settled on her comfy sofa, which faced both a cheery gas fireplace and big windows that looked out over the ocean.

They chatted and laughed for about an hour before

Marley suggested that they pick a movie to watch on Netflix. She was about to flick the TV on and start scrolling through the options when Mark's expression changed. He took the remote from her and set it down next to him, which completely confused her.

"I want to watch a movie, but there's something I need to ask you first." There was a funny, nervous tone to his voice as he reached in his pocket, stood, then got down on one knee. And then she realized what was going on.

"Marley. Meeting you has been an unexpected joy. At this point in my life, I didn't think I'd find love again. And I've found so much more than that with you. I love that we're great friends and you're the one I want to spend time with. I know this is kind of fast, but when you know, you know. Will you marry me?" He looked at her and the love in his eyes brought tears to her own.

She looked down at the ring. It was beautiful, a generously sized diamond on a delicate platinum band with a circle of smaller diamonds around it. She loved it. And she loved him. But she wasn't anywhere near ready to get married. She took a deep breath.

"Mark, I love you. So much. And this ring is beautiful. It's perfect. I love what we have. But, I'm so sorry that I can't say yes right now. I'm just not ready to get married again. Not yet. I'm not sure when I will be. But I know that I want to be with you. I hope you can understand. It's not because I don't love you."

The light in his eyes dimmed as he nodded. "I know this is fast. I'd hoped that it wouldn't matter, and you'd want to take the leap with me. But, I probably should have felt you out first. We haven't really talked about marriage."

"No, we haven't," she agreed. "If we had, I would have told you it's just not something I'm in a hurry to do again. Not after being married for over thirty years. I haven't even been divorced for a year yet. It's a big change."

Mark was quiet for a long moment, before trying again. "We wouldn't have to set a date. We could have a really long engagement. Would that help?" He sounded so earnest that it broke her heart. But she just couldn't go there yet.

She shook her head sadly. "I just can't say yes to marriage yet. Even with a long engagement. I'm really sorry. Can we just enjoy what we have? I don't want anything to change."

Mark nodded, closed the ring box and put it back in his pant pocket. Marley reached out and grabbed his free hand and gave it a gentle squeeze, then pulled him in for a kiss—a passionate one to show him how she really felt. When they finished, she looked into his eyes. "I really do love you, you know."

He smiled. "I know you do."

MARLEY FELT RESTLESS THE NEXT DAY. NORMALLY MARK would have stayed over but after she refused his proposal and he said that he understood, once they finished watching the movie, he surprised her by saying he was tired and was going to head home.

She couldn't help second-guessing herself. Was she being crazy to insist on waiting? Did he have a point and they could just have a long engagement? Her gut response was no, and that it was just too soon. But still, she felt badly about it. She wanted to talk to Lisa, to see what she thought and hopefully to get reassurance that she'd done the right thing.

She knew that Lisa often had her family over for Sunday dinner mid-day, so she didn't want to interrupt that. So, she waited until four before calling. Lisa picked up on the first ring.

"I hope you're not in the middle of dinner with the family? I can call back later," Marley said.

Lisa laughed. "No, you're not interrupting anything. I was actually feeling a little stir-crazy. It's quiet here. I don't have any guests until later in the week and Rhett had to go into the restaurant as his manager is sick. And the kids were all busy. I was just sitting here debating what to do for dinner."

"Do you want to go grab a bite somewhere? I had a situation last night with Mark that I'd love your advice on."

"Well, that sounds intriguing. Yes, I'd love to. We could go to Rhett's restaurant—he told me what the specials are and they sound fantastic."

"Perfect. What time do you want to meet there?"

"How about at five? We can eat at the bar. If I get there before you, I'll grab seats for us."

MARLEY ARRIVED AT RHETT'S RIGHT AT FIVE AND SMILED when she saw that Lisa was already sitting at the bar, chatting with Rhett. It was early, so the restaurant wasn't busy yet and there were only two others at the bar. She slid into the seat next to Lisa. Rhett nodded hello and left a moment later to head back into the kitchen.

Lisa turned to Marley and smiled. "I'm so glad we did this. I actually haven't been here in ages."

The bartender, a dark-haired man close to their age, came right over and Lisa introduced him. "Marley, this is Jose. I think I'm going to have something different. Rhett says Jose makes the best margaritas."

"That sounds good to me. I'll have one too."

Jose went off to make their drinks and Lisa shared, "Rhett said he was lucky to get Jose. He has quite a following and was only available because the restaurant he was working for closed unexpectedly. "

Jose returned and set their drinks down. Marley took a sip, and it was unusually good. She tried to place what it was that was different.

"This is delicious. What's your secret?" She asked him.

Jose looked pleased. "Thank you. It's a splash of fresh-squeezed orange juice."

Two more customers came to the bar, and Jose wandered off to help them. Lisa lifted her glass and tapped it against Marley's. "Cheers! Now, fill me in. What's going on?"

Marley told her all the details of the night before. Lisa listened quietly, sipping her margarita as Marley described the proposal and Marley's refusal. When she finished, Lisa was quiet for a moment before saying, "My heart goes out to him. But, you hadn't discussed marriage before this, did you?"

"Not once. And we'd only just said I love you very recently and broke up before that. It was completely unexpected."

Lisa nodded. "I think it's really sweet of him. But, I wouldn't feel at all bad about saying no. If you feel like it's too soon, then it's too soon. How did he take it?"

"He said he understood, but I could tell he was disappointed. It's a big deal to give someone a ring—and then have them say no. He went home after we watched a movie. Said he was tired."

Lisa raised an eyebrow. "Maybe he just needed to process the no."

"Probably so. So you don't think it was awful of me to say no?"

"It wasn't awful. You were married for a long time and it hasn't even been a year since you divorced, right?"

"Right."

"It's not like you are saying no to him. Just no to getting engaged right now."

Marley liked the sound of that and relaxed a little. She realized she'd been tense all day, worrying about how Mark was feeling.

"We do love each other. I reminded him of that and

just said I wasn't ready yet. I don't know when I will be. I'm just happy spending time with him."

"Well, if you told him all that, then I really and truly wouldn't worry," Lisa assured her.

"Thank you. I was hoping you'd say that."

"Absolutely. Now, what are we going to eat?"

CHAPTER 27

"Good morning, Taylor! Shall I pour you a cup?" Blake's father was full of energy as he poured himself a cup of coffee Tuesday morning. She'd gone in a little earlier than usual to prepare for her interview with Philippe Gaston. It was a few minutes past eight and they were the only two in the office.

"Yes, please. Thank you." She gratefully took the steaming mug of hot black coffee from him and turned to head to her desk.

"You're in bright and early today. Busy day?" He asked, looking at her curiously.

She smiled. "I have an interview with a local author this morning, Philippe Gaston. I wanted to go over my notes a bit before heading out."

"I've read a few of his books. Good storyteller. I'll keep an eye out for that interview." He headed off to his office and Taylor settled at her desk and jumped online to do some last-minute research. She read over as many prior interviews as she could find, as well as press announcements of Philippe's upcoming deals and releases. She didn't want to cover things that were either easily available by a google search or had already been asked in prior interviews. She was a big fan of his books, so she had a list of questions she wanted to ask and added a few more to the list as she did her research.

Forty-five minutes later, she packed up to head to Philippe's house. She downed the last sip of coffee, which was now ice cold, and threw her laptop and notebook in her tote bag. She was still the only person in the office other than Blake's father, but as she walked out the front door, she heard footsteps behind her.

"Taylor!" She turned at the sound of Blake's voice.

"Morning." She smiled at Richard, who was right behind Blake, his tail wagging. Blake hadn't shaved and had a slight stubble shadow and it looked good on him. She glanced away.

"Are you off to see Philippe?"

She nodded. "We're set to talk at nine."

"Good luck then. I'll see you when you get back."

TAYLOR PUT PHILIPPE'S ADDRESS INTO HER GPS, EVEN though she had a good idea where the street was. During one of her visits, Abby had taken her for a driving tour of the island and they went everywhere, and marveled at many of the seaside mansions with their multi-million dollar views. It amazed Taylor that so many were second homes and sat empty most of the year, waiting for their owners to visit.

She recognized Philippe's street as one of the water-front ones and when she turned onto it and then pulled into his driveway, she was impressed. His home was large and lovely, with an expansive lawn and overlooked the ocean with lots of big glass windows.

She parked, grabbed her bag and walked to the front door, and rang the bell. A moment later, the door opened and a pretty blonde woman welcomed her.

"Hi, I'm Angela. Are you from the paper?"

"Yes, I'm Taylor Abbott."

"Come on in. Philippe is in his office. Would you like some coffee?"

"No, thank you though." She followed Angela through the sunny home with its wide hardwood floors and high cathedral ceilings that let in lots of light. It felt like the house was literally on the water because the views from every window were of nothing but ocean. They passed by the kitchen, which was state-of-the-art. Angela led her into a large office with even more breathtaking views of the harbor.

The walls were lined with book cases that overflowed with everything from Philippe's own, to other bestsellers and classic leather-bound books. Philippe was sitting behind a desk that was a thick, heavy slab of glass. He stood to welcome them and invited Taylor to sit in one of the two leather chairs facing the desk. Angela sat in the other one.

"Thanks for coming out. Do you mind if Angela sits

in on this? I thought we could chat a little about her background too."

Taylor smiled. "Of course."

They talked about Philippe first. Taylor asked about his upcoming releases and movies.

"Do you like the film versions that have been made of your books so far?" Taylor knew that most people usually felt that, in general, books were better than the movies based on them.

"So far, yes. I'm lucky though as I've been able to be fairly involved, both with the screenplay writing and I even had some input on casting. I used to spend quite a bit of time in LA."

"Are you spending less time now?"

He nodded. "Yes. Once Angela and I decided to get married, that was one of the things I wanted to cut back on. I didn't want to be gone for weeks—or more often—months at a time. I may still do future film deals but won't be as involved on site."

"How did the two of you meet?" Taylor always loved hearing about how people met and fell in love.

Philippe glanced at Angela. "Do you want to take this?"

She laughed. "Sure. So, when I came to Nantucket, it was just supposed to be a temporary thing. I'd inherited a cottage from a grandmother I never knew and it needed some work done before I could sell it, so I stayed at The Beach Plum Cove Inn while the work was being done."

"I stayed there too! Lisa's daughter, Abby, was my college roommate."

Angela smiled. "I got to know Abby, and Kristen and Kate. I'd worked as a maid in California and was helping Lisa out a bit at the inn. Then Kate's friend Philippe needed someone to clean this house, and that's how we met. I wasn't looking for any kind of relationship."

"I didn't think that I was either," Philippe admitted. "My track record wasn't very good. I was great at dating, but not at anything long-term or serious. Until I met Angela."

"We hit it off immediately, but as friends," Angela added.

Philippe grinned. "I always wanted to be more than friends."

"I still thought living here was going to be a temporary thing. And everyone warned me that Philippe wasn't boyfriend material—even though they all loved him."

"I won her over, though. And convinced her to stay."

"He did. I was still going to college, for marketing and thought I had to move home to finish that too. But I realized that I didn't want a career in marketing, and that I could finish school online."

"So, she started her own cleaning business and used what she learned about marketing to grow the business," Philippe said proudly.

"I actually really enjoy cleaning," Angela admitted. "So, it made sense to make a business out of it. And it's worked out pretty well so far."

"She's being modest. Sales have grown, and she just hired two new cleaners," Philippe said.

Angela laughed. "He's my biggest cheerleader. But

things are going well. What about you? Do you think you'll stay on the island for a while? I can't imagine living anywhere else now."

"I hope it works out that I can stay here for a very long time. I haven't lived here long, but it already feels like home to me. And I'm loving working at the paper."

Philippe nodded. "Blake's a good guy. I've known him for a while. He's a good writer too, though I haven't seen anything from him in the paper for a while."

Taylor hadn't seen anything from Blake either since she'd joined the paper.

"He might be too busy managing things. He hired another reporter that started a week or two before I did."

"That could be it. Tell him I said he needs to write something, though. He had some great opinion pieces. He's a sharp guy. But you obviously know that if you work for him."

Taylor smiled. "He is. He's good at trivia too. A bunch of us play every week at the Rose and Crown."

Angela and Philippe exchanged glances.

"I love trivia," Angela said. "We should go again sometime. We haven't been in ages."

"We could. That's always a fun time."

"You could join our team. Blake is always saying the more the merrier."

Philippe grinned. "Well, count us in then."

CHAPTER 28

Energy was high in the newsroom when Taylor walked in. Victoria was on the phone doing an interview and Joe was talking to Blake's father. He was standing by his desk, holding his laptop, so Taylor wasn't sure if he was coming or going. Richard came wandering over to say hello and, as she reached over to pet him, Taylor glanced around the office but didn't see Blake. After a moment, Richard headed back to Blake's office, and she guessed that's where Blake was.

She settled at her desk, pulled out her notes from the interview with Philippe, and started working on her story. She didn't look up again until half past noon when she clicked send and emailed her story to Blake. She stood and stretched, her muscles tight from sitting in the same position for so long as she focused on her work. She was pleased with how the interview turned out and hoped that Blake would like it. Now that she was done, she was starving and decided to walk over to Oath Pizza down on the wharf and get a slice or two of pizza for lunch. It was quick and delicious.

She smiled as Richard came over again to say hello, but this time, Blake was with him. She scratched the dog behind his ears and sighed.

"I think it might be time for me to get a dog. Do you know of any places I should go to on Nantucket to adopt one?"

Blake's face lit up. "You want a dog? That's a great idea. You can bring it in, you know."

"I know. I'm not sure I would get one otherwise. I'd feel bad being gone all day, but I love that I can bring the dog to work with me."

Blake nodded. "I felt the same way. It's worked out pretty good so far. What are you doing right now?"

"I was going to grab a slice of pizza at Oath."

"Want to make a stop first? We can go there on the way back."

"Okay.." Taylor wasn't sure where he wanted to go.

He grinned. "We can go to the animal shelter. It's where I got Richard. You won't be able to take the dog home today, but you can get the process started. If you're serious about it?"

"Oh! Yes, I'm serious. I'd love to do that." She'd been thinking about getting a dog since before she moved into the cottage. Taylor loved it there, but it was very quiet— she missed the energy of being at the inn. So, she was looking forward to having another presence in the house. And she loved the idea of bringing the dog to work.

When she'd signed the lease for the cottage, Mr. Rugby had said then that a small cat or dog would be allowed. She'd always had pets growing up, and she still missed Peaches, the family dog that passed less than a year ago.

"Okay, let me grab my keys and we can go. The shelter is maybe a five-minute drive." Blake got Richard settled with a bowl of dry food in his office and he and Taylor headed out.

They reached the shelter a few minutes later and the woman at the front desk smiled when she recognized Blake.

"Blake, nice to see you. Is Richard okay? Or are you interested in getting another dog?"

"Hey, Janie. Richard's good. It's actually my friend Taylor that's interested."

"Oh, well, that's great. We can head out back so you can see the dogs. If you find one you like, we have some paperwork that has to be processed. We check a vet reference which usually takes a day or two, and there's a small fee for the vet check and any spaying. After that, you can come and take your dog home. Sound good?"

"Yes, perfect."

"Okay, follow me." Janie led them down a hallway and into a large room where a dozen or so dogs of all sizes and ages were in big crates. Taylor's heart went out to all of them and she wished she could take them all home. She loved getting pets from shelters, but she hated this part, having to choose. Sometimes, though, the animals did the choosing. And that was the case today.

She and Blake walked along, saying hello to all the

dogs. They were all cute, but when they reached the last one, Taylor felt a pull. This dog was smaller than the others and eyed them warily with a resigned yet oddly hopeful look in its big brown eyes.

"What kind of dog is this?" Taylor asked. The dog was very small, with big ears and a fur coat that was pretty mix of chestnut and white.

Janie smiled. "That's Patricia. We call her Miss Pat. She's a Cavalier King Charles Spaniel. She's a sweetheart. She's been here for quite a while."

That explained the sad look in the dog's eyes. "Why is she here? And why hasn't she been adopted?"

"Well, she's older. She's almost eight. Her owner passed away. Most people want younger dogs. They always go first. But these dogs typically live to be 12-15 years on average. She should have a lot of life left."

Taylor leaned over and gently put her hand through the holes of the crate. "Hi Patricia…." The little dog cocked her head and stared at her for a moment before tentatively walking over and rubbing her cheek against Taylor's hand. And Taylor's heart immediately melted. After a moment, she stood up.

"I'd like to take her."

Janie looked surprised. "You want Patricia? Really? Are you sure?"

Taylor nodded. "I'm sure."

Janie's eyes watered. "Well, that's just wonderful. We've been so hopeful that she'd find the right owner. Come with me and we'll get your paperwork started."

Blake nodded his approval. "She's cute."

Taylor filled out the forms and wrote out a check to cover Patricia's adoption fee.

"We'll put a call into your vet today and as soon as we hear back, we'll give you a call to schedule a time to come pick her up," Janie said.

———————

"YOU GOT YOURSELF A DOG!" BLAKE LOOKED PLEASED AS they climbed into his Jeep and headed back toward the office. They stopped at Oath to pick up pizza slices for lunch. It didn't take long, and they chatted in line as they waited.

"How'd the interview go with Philippe?" Blake asked.

"Good, I think. I talked to his wife, Angela, too. I emailed it to you right before we left."

"Excellent. I'll look it over this afternoon. He's a good friend. We met a few years ago. He used to play trivia with us now and then. It's been a while though."

"I mentioned it to him, actually. He and Angela might join us this week."

"No kidding? That would be great. The more the merrier."

Taylor smiled. "I told him you'd say that."

They took their pizzas back to the office and Blake headed to his desk and Taylor did the same. Victoria raised her eyebrows when the two of them walked in together, and as soon as Blake walked away, she turned her chair to face Taylor.

"What are you two up to? You left in a hurry."

"Blake took me to the animal shelter. I found a dog I want to adopt."

The look of surprise on Victoria's face almost made Taylor laugh. She clearly was not expecting that.

"Really? You're getting a dog? Why?" It was no surprise that Victoria was not an animal lover.

"I love dogs. I've been wanting to get one for a while."

"I thought you were off doing something more interesting than that. Animals are so much work."

"I take it you don't have pets?"

"Me? No. Todd wants one, but I've been discouraging that. I do have news, though. I'm getting closer to an interview with Wesley Stevens!"

"You are? How?"

"Todd and I like The Gaslight and our waitress told us Saturday night when we went for dinner, that Wes has been in a few times. He likes the music I guess."

"Really? That's surprising. He doesn't get mobbed?"

"She said he disguises himself. Wears a baseball cap and dark glasses. But he's come in a few times now, so she's onto him."

"I'm surprised she told you," Taylor said.

Victoria grinned. "Well, we tip well, and she knows I've been on the hunt. I told her if I get an interview, there's a big tip in it for her."

"That's resourceful of you." It never would have occurred to Taylor to do any of that.

"I told you, I'm getting an interview with him. It's happening!"

Taylor laughed. She wished she had half of Victoria's confidence. "I hope it works out for you."

"Thanks. It will, you'll see."

CHAPTER 29

"Don't be nervous." Rhett had a feeling he knew what was bothering Lisa. They were sitting at breakfast. The dining room was quiet, as there was just one couple staying at the inn and they hadn't come down to eat yet. Lisa had a plate of fluffy scrambled eggs and bacon and he was sipping his first cup of coffee, watching her frown as she stared out the window. She was a million miles away.

She brought her attention back to him and smiled. "What makes you think I'm nervous?"

"I can tell you're worrying. Today's the first day that the orders are going to the new bakers. It will be fine." They'd gone there the week before and met with the team that was going to bake the quiches. They were experienced and capable and Rhett had thoroughly vetted them, checking references from people he knew in the industry.

"How did you know?" Lisa looked surprised.

He laughed. "I know you. I've also run a few businesses myself and it's scary giving control over to other people. But it's how you grow. You have to trust them—until you have a reason not to."

Lisa nodded. "You're right. I know you're right."

"Sometimes you get burned. Like I did with the twins. But it doesn't happen often. And it's not going to happen to you. When are you going to turn up the marketing?"

"Marley suggested that we wait a few weeks. To make sure things are going smoothly and then increase the ads by twenty-five percent."

Rhett nodded. "That sounds like a good plan."

"She also invited us to dinner this Saturday. She's having her first dinner party. Sue and Paige are going too."

"I'll make sure I head home before the dinner rush on Saturday, then." Rhett usually went in on Saturday during the day to make sure they were all set for the evening shift. Occasionally he worked a Saturday night, but he mostly worked days so he could spend his nights at home with Lisa. Having a good management team in place helped with that.

"Good, I'll let her know we'll be there. It should be fun." Lisa looked more relaxed now.

"I'm sure it will be." Rhett finished his coffee and stood. Lisa's eggs looked good, and he was ready to go get some for himself.

"Any word from the shelter yet?" Blake asked as he walked by Taylor's desk Thursday morning. Richard was right behind him.

"No word yet." Taylor was a little concerned that she hadn't heard anything. "Should I be worried? My vet reference should be fine."

"Maybe they haven't connected with your vet yet. I wouldn't worry. I'm sure you'll be approved."

Blake fumbled around in his stack of mail, looking for something. "You're in for trivia tonight, right? Looks like we might have a good group going. Philippe texted that he and Angela will meet us there."

"Yes, I'm in. Looking forward to it."

Blake found what he was looking for and handed her a copy of the newest edition of the paper. "Check it out. Your feature on Philippe made the front page. I'll catch up with you later." He and Richard headed to his office.

Taylor glanced at the paper in surprise. She knew Philippe was well known, but she hadn't expected that her article would make the front page. Blake had told her it turned out well though, and it was a long, detailed interview. Her phone rang and when she saw that it was her dad, she smiled. She'd save him a copy of the paper. He'd love seeing that her article made the front page, and she knew he was a fan of Philippe's books, too.

"Hi Dad, what's up?"

"Good morning! I know you're working, so I won't keep you. I just wanted to double-check before I book the ferry—next weekend is still good for me to come visit?"

"Yes! And hopefully you'll meet my new family member by then. I'm adopting a dog."

"You always did like dogs. Okay, honey, I'll book this and plan to see you next Friday evening. I think I get into Nantucket around five."

"Great. I'll meet you at the wharf when you get in."

"Okay, I'm booked! I'll let you get back to work now. Love you!"

Taylor smiled. "I love you too, Dad."

THE REST OF THE DAY FLEW, AND JUST AS TAYLOR WAS getting ready to head out to trivia, her phone rang.

"Taylor? This is Janie at the shelter. I'm sorry it took a few days to get back to you, but your vet was out of town. We just connected and I'm happy to say that you are approved to adopt Patricia. You can come anytime tomorrow to get her. Just give us a call before you come so we will have her ready for you."

"Thank you! I will." Taylor was still smiling when Blake walked over. He'd just returned from bringing Richard home and walking and feeding him before he left.

"Are you guys ready to head over for trivia?" He asked. Joe was already heading their way. Taylor stood and grabbed her purse.

"I'm ready."

"You look happy about something," Blake commented as they walked out together.

"The shelter just called. I can pick up Patricia tomorrow."

"Oh, that's great. If you want, why don't you work from home tomorrow? Then you can get her settled in over the weekend."

"Really? That would be awesome." Taylor still needed to run to the store to pick up dog food, bowls, a dog bed and anything else Patricia might need. She could get up early and go on her way to the shelter.

Mary and Emily joined them and their group of five made their way over to the Rose and Crown. Blake asked for a bigger table than usual and a few minutes later, Angela and Philippe joined them.

Blake sat next to Taylor and Angela slid into the empty seat on Taylor's other side. Blake introduced everyone and Owen, the trivia host, came by a moment later to say hello and hand out the answer pads and score-sheets for the night.

"I saw the article today. It turned out great. Philippe was thrilled to be on the front page," Angela said.

"Thanks. I was excited to see that too."

"I loved the article, Taylor," Philippe said. He turned to Blake and grinned. "You should promote her!"

Blake laughed. "I'll keep that in mind."

When their waitress came around, they put their food and drinks order in. She returned a few minutes later with their drinks. They all shared a plate of nachos and some fried calamari while they waited for their meals. Taylor and Blake both got smokehouse burgers, big burgers topped with bacon, cheese and barbecue sauce.

"That looks good." Angela eyed their burgers as the waitress set down her sensible salad with grilled chicken. "I might have to get that next time."

Taylor laughed. "It is really good. We order it almost every time now."

"You look like an old married couple, with your matching meals," Philippe teased them.

Taylor glanced around the table. Joe, Mary and Emily were laughing about something else while Blake was busy pouring ketchup on his burger and didn't react at all to what Philippe said.

Angela shot her husband a look. "Ignore him. He hasn't gotten out much lately. He's forgotten how to behave."

Philippe laughed. "She's right. This is our first night out in ages. I've been buried with finishing a book. But it's done now and I can relax and play for a bit."

Soon after they finished eating, Owen announced the first trivia question, and they were off and running. It was definitely more fun with more people on the team and livelier too, as they didn't always agree on what the best answer was. But Philippe knew a few answers that the rest of them were totally stuck on and Angela turned out to be great with science questions.

When they got to the final question, Owen announced that the category was movies.

"Taylor, this one's for you," Blake said. Which made her a little nervous. She usually did well on the entertainment questions but also knew that the final questions were the most difficult.

"Okay, here we go," Owen said dramatically. He had a gleam in his eye that didn't make Taylor any less nervous. "What Film Was So Scary Theatre Staff Supposedly Carried Smelling Salts For Guests?"

Smelling salts! Taylor hadn't a clue. She'd never been into scary movies.

"What do you think, Taylor?" Blake asked.

"I honestly have no idea. The Exorcist maybe?"

"Texas Chainsaw Massacre?" Philippe suggested.

Blake looked around the table. Mary, Joe and Emily just shook their heads.

"I have no idea either," He said. "Angela, any thoughts?"

Angela smiled. "I actually think I know this one. I'm pretty sure it's The Phantom of the Opera."

Philippe looked doubtful. "I don't know. That doesn't seem all that scary compared to the other two we mentioned."

"I'm not at all sure of my answer. It was just a guess," Taylor said quickly.

"I'm not sure either," Philippe admitted.

"Think about it logically," Angela said. "Smelling salts are from a different era. Lon Chaney's Phantom was pretty terrifying for its time. And it was long before the other two."

Blake nodded. "That makes sense to me. Let's go with it."

He turned in their answer and a few minutes later, Owen announced that they were the only team that got it right, and that took them from third place to first. They were the overall winners for the night.

"That's my wife!" Philippe said proudly as everyone high-fived Angela.

Once they paid the bill, they all walked out together and said goodbye to Angela and Philippe.

"That was so fun. Do you guys come every week?" Angela asked.

Blake nodded. "Every week. Join us whenever you can. Hopefully we'll see you next week, maybe?"

"Sounds good to me," Philippe said as he and Angela headed in the opposite direction.

The walk back to the office only took a few minutes. Mary, Emily and Joe walked in front of them, laughing at something Joe said. Taylor and Blake weren't quite close enough to hear what they were talking about.

Blake turned to her with a question.

"Any big plans for the weekend?"

"None. Just settling in with Patricia. What about you?"

"My mother is having a dinner tomorrow night that I promised to attend. Other than that, not much going on. Maybe I'll stop by Saturday afternoon and see how you and Patricia are getting along?"

"Sure, that would be great. I don't really want to leave her this weekend."

"Right. She needs to get used to the new place. See how she's doing and maybe by Monday you can bring her in—for part of the day, anyway. Ease her in slowly."

"That's a great idea," Taylor agreed.

They reached the office and everyone went their separate ways.

"I'll be online all day tomorrow if you need to reach me. And of course I'll have my cell." Taylor said.

Blake smiled. "I know where to find you. Good luck with Patricia."

It was a fun night and as Taylor drove home, she couldn't help thinking about what Philippe said earlier. She and Blake were so comfortable together, laughing and joking as they all tried to come up with the right answers. They even finished each other's sentences at times. And now and then she got a certain feeling, when he smiled at her or held her gaze a moment longer than he needed to, that if he wasn't her boss, maybe there could be something to explore there. But she also knew that shouldn't happen.

CHAPTER 30

Taylor called the shelter as soon as they opened the next day and told them she'd be by around eleven to pick up Patricia. She stopped by Geronimo's Pet Store on her way there and got everything she needed, a comfy dog bed, a cute set of bowls for food and water, and plenty of food. Janie at the shelter told her what they'd been feeding her, so she made sure to get some of the same food to help her acclimate.

When she arrived at the shelter, Janie was happy to see her.

"I'll bring Patricia right out. I think she knows she's going home today. She's been in an unusually good mood." She left and returned a few moments later, leading Patricia by a pink leash, which she handed to Taylor. "Here you go. She's all yours now. I hope you'll be very happy together."

"Thank you." Taylor bent down and carefully petted

Patricia, who looked up at her with those big, soulful brown eyes. "Let's go home."

She led the dog to her car and opened the door to the backseat and Patricia hopped in and flopped down on the seat. Taylor closed the door carefully behind her and drove home. Patricia was quiet the whole way and each time that Taylor stole a glance at her in the rear-view mirror, she was gazing out the window and seemed pretty relaxed about it all.

When she reached the cottage, Taylor took Patricia for a walk around the yard for a few minutes. She happily did her business by a bush, and then Taylor led her inside and ran back to the car to bring in all of her supplies. She set the dog bed by the sofa and filled her bowls with dry food and fresh water. Patricia walked around the room, sniffing everything, including the food. She took a sip of water, then went and curled up on her dog bed as if she'd been doing it forever. So far, she was definitely a mellow dog, which Taylor appreciated.

She got her laptop out and sat on the sofa by Patricia, who lifted her head and watched Taylor for a moment before closing her eyes and drifting off to sleep. The rest of the day was uneventful, and Taylor got a lot of work done. She took Patricia out for walks several times and was glad to see that she had a healthy appetite as she ate quite a bit of the food in her bowl.

Later that evening, when she was ready to go to bed, Patricia cocked her head and watched as Taylor went upstairs. She wasn't up there for more than a few minutes, and was just changing into her pajamas and brushing her teeth, when Patricia started to bark and to whine. She sounded upset. Taylor went downstairs to see what was the matter and saw the dog at the foot of the stairs looking up with a distressed expression. She barked again when she saw Taylor.

"Do you want to come upstairs, too?" Taylor went and got her dog bed and went to bring it upstairs. She took one step and looked back at Patricia. "Come on up, it's okay."

Patricia followed her upstairs and as soon as Taylor set the dog bed down, Patricia stepped into it, walked around in a circle a few times and then settled herself. Taylor made a mental note to pick up another dog bed so she could leave one upstairs.

BLAKE WAS STARTING TO REGRET THAT HE'D AGREED TO have dinner at his parents' house Friday night. His mother had called him twice that afternoon to confirm and the second time she called, she told him to make sure he wore something presentable. And there was something about her tone that made him question her.

"Since when do you care what I wear?"

"I just haven't seen you all dressed up in a while. You look so nice when you wear a button-down shirt and a tie." She used the sugary sweet tone she only used when she was trying to get her way about something.

"Mom, I love you, but I'm not wearing a shirt and tie to have dinner with you and Dad at home."

There was a long pause. "Well, just do your best, dear. We'll see you at six."

At the end of the day, Blake took Richard for a long walk and then brought him upstairs to get him settled before he headed out. He glanced at himself in the mirror. He was wearing jeans, and a faded Nantucket Red button-down shirt that he'd bought a few months ago because he liked the color. He thought it looked fine enough for dinner with his parents, and he wasn't inclined to change. He certainly wasn't adding a tie.

He stopped at Bradford's Liquors along the way and picked up a good bottle of pinot noir for his mother. He wasn't sure what she was serving, but Belle Glos was her favorite wine, so maybe she'd overlook his attire if he brought her wine she loved.

He arrived at five past six and was surprised to see an unfamiliar car in the driveway. He let himself in and as he made his way toward the kitchen, he heard a familiar voice—yet it was surprising to hear that voice here. What was his mother up to?

He stepped into the kitchen and his mother broke into a big smile when she saw him.

"Oh good, Blake is here. Blake, you remember Andi of course and her mother Muriel? I've been meaning to have them over for ages. I'm so glad it worked out that everyone was available tonight." So this was why his mother wanted him to dress up. Blake sighed. He did not like being manipulated.

"Nice to see you again," Muriel said. She leaned in and kissed his cheek.

"You too," Blake said. "And Andi." He gave her a hug hello.

His father leaned against the kitchen counter and took it all in. Blake handed him the bottle of wine.

"Here you go. It's mom's favorite."

His mother's eyes lit up. "Belle Glos? How thoughtful. Let's open it now. It will go well with the pâte I picked up earlier at Nantucket Meat and Fish. Gerry will take care of that for us."

Blake's father nodded. "I'm on it." He found the wine opener, opened the wine and poured some for everyone, while his mother set a dish with the pâte and baguette slices on the kitchen island. She also set out a bowl with some kind of hummus and tortilla chips.

"What's for dinner, Mom?" Something smelled good, but his mother had never been much of a cook. She was very good at ordering takeout though, and they'd always gone out to dinner often.

"We're having prime rib, baked potatoes and green beans."

"Impressive." Blake wondered where she'd ordered it from.

"How's your father?" Blake asked Andi. He was surprised that he hadn't joined them.

"He's good. He had a golf thing with some of his friends."

"Andi, Blake mentioned you were both going to that book talk the other night, to see that mystery writer?" His mother said. "I don't recall his name. Was it fun?"

Andi smiled. "Philippe Gaston. Yes, it was a nice

event. I went with my sister Kelly, and we ran into Blake and his employee—Taylor, right?"

He nodded. "Yes, Taylor. It was a good time. She did a follow-up interview with Philippe this week that turned out great. Made the front page."

"How nice." His mother flashed her super sweet smile before turning her attention back to Andi. "Your mother was telling me that your father is planning to move the business back here year-round. Will you be joining them?"

Andi nodded. "I think so. Though I did really enjoy Florida, especially in the winter."

"It's unusual for people to leave Nantucket and then decide they want to come back permanently," Blake said. He'd be willing to bet that Andi would find a way to stay in Florida most of the time. She hadn't been back on the island more than a handful of times over the past few years. It didn't seem like she missed it that much.

"I don't think it's that unusual," his mother said.

Blake helped himself to some of the pâte, which was very good, while his mother steered the conversation where she wanted it to go. Eventually, she suggested they all move into the dining room. He helped her bring the food in, carrying a platter of carved prime rib while his father followed with the vegetables.

The food was good, and the conversation was tolerable until they finished eating and his mother not so subtly brought up the fact that both he and Andi were very much single at the moment.

"You two should spend more time together," she

suggested, with a wide-eyed smile, as if the thought had just innocently crossed her mind.

"I'm sure Blake is very busy," Andi protested, which left him no choice, unless he wanted to seem like a jerk.

"Not too busy at all. We should do that," he said.

"Excellent. Why don't the two of you take a walk outside and make a plan while we clear the table?" His mother suggested.

Andi glanced at him and it was clear she felt as awkward as he did.

"Yes, you two run along. Come back in five minutes or so for dessert. We brought a cheesecake," Andi's mother said.

That left them no choice. "Let's go take a walk," Blake said. He led the way outside to the back deck and his parents' patio and garden area.

"I'm so sorry about that," Andi said.

"You have nothing to apologize for. I can pretty much guarantee this was all my mother's idea. She's been relentless since Caroline and I decided not to get married."

Andi looked sympathetic. "I know that wasn't all that long ago. I'm sure dating might not even be on your mind, yet."

"It really hasn't been. But I probably should start thinking about it at some point. As my mother likes to remind me, it has been six months."

"And we are both single now," Andi said.

"So, should we make everyone happy and set a date

to go out? We can do dinner or drinks or both, whatever you want?"

"How about Millie's next weekend?" Andi suggested.

Blake liked the sound of that. Millie's was a casual Mexican restaurant on the ocean. A great spot for drinks and a bite to eat. "That sounds good to me. How about Saturday at six?"

"It's a date," she said.

Blake grinned. "Okay, ready to go in and give them the good news?"

Andi laughed. "Yes. Let's go make their night."

CHAPTER 31

Taylor woke around three in the morning to the sound of Patricia whimpering in her sleep and kicking her feet around. She got up and went over to her and spoke softly.

"It's okay. You're just having a bad dream. You're home now." The whimpering slowed. She reached out and gently patted Patricia's head until it stopped completely, and the restless feet stilled. Taylor waited a few more moments, then climbed back into bed and fell fast asleep.

When she woke in the morning a little past seven, Patricia was already up and waiting at the top of the stairs, her tail twitching. She turned at the sound of Taylor getting out of bed and her tail started going faster.

"Good morning. I'm guessing you want to go outside?" Taylor laughed as she went downstairs, Patricia right behind her. She found her leash, and they went outside for a walk.

The rest of the day was uneventful and busy. Taylor did errands around the house most of the day, including several loads of laundry. It was a relaxing day overall, and Patricia seemed to be settling in nicely. She was content to follow Taylor around the cottage, go for several walks, and nap in between.

And Taylor took a little more care with how she dressed. Instead of wearing sweats like she normally would on a Saturday, she chose her favorite pink sweater and a pair of old, but flattering jeans, just in case Blake stopped by.

But by a quarter to five there was no sign of him, and she wondered if it was just something he'd said in passing. Maybe he was too busy. She was starting to feel a bit hungry and wondered what she might make for dinner when suddenly there was a knock on the door. She hadn't even heard a car pull into the driveway, but when she glanced out the window, she saw the familiar gray Jeep.

She opened the door and Blake stood there holding a cardboard pizza box. The tantalizing smell of the cheese and tomato sauce made her stomach rumble. She opened the door wide to let him in. He stepped inside and handed her the box.

"I didn't want to come empty-handed, and I figured you might be busy with Patricia and might not feel like cooking."

Taylor laughed. "Thank you. I was just thinking about what to do for dinner. This is perfect. She opened the box and took a look at the pizza inside. It was pepperoni and looked delicious. "Are you hungry? Should we eat this now?"

Blake smiled. "I'm always hungry. How is Patricia doing?" He looked around the room and saw the dog curled up in her bed by the sofa.

"Good, so far. Go say hello while I get this ready for us."

Taylor got some plates out of the cupboard and put a couple of pizza slices on each one. Meanwhile, Blake chatted with Patricia, who seemed to love the attention.

"What would you like to drink?" Taylor looked in her refrigerator. "I have Diet Coke, Chardonnay, or water."

"What are you having?"

"I think I might have a glass of Chardonnay."

"Then I'll have the same."

Taylor poured two glasses and set them on the counter. Blake came over a moment later and they brought their wine and pizza over to the sofa and sat by Patricia. She sniffed the air and looked at them both hopefully.

"No, sorry you're not getting pizza, my dear," Taylor said. Patricia shook her head and settled back into position.

"She looks like she's right at home," Blake said

Taylor smiled. "She's great. So far she seems like she's adjusting nicely."

The pizza tasted as good as it smelled and hit the spot. They chatted for a few minutes before Taylor asked, "How was your dinner with the parents last night?"

Blake made a face. "It was interesting. My mother was up to her scheming antics again."

"What do you mean?"

"She likes to play matchmaker. My sister is married, I was almost married and ever since that fell through, she's been anxious about getting me paired up again."

Taylor laughed. "What did she do?"

"Well, apparently she decided that she'd like me to be dating Andi again. You remember her from the book event?"

Taylor nodded. "I remember."

"Well, she invited Andi and her mother to dinner but she didn't tell me that she invited either of them. So it was totally a setup and a bit awkward. To make a long story short, I now have a date with Andi next Saturday night."

Taylor laughed. "And that's a bad thing?"

Blake sighed. "Andi is great, but we already dated briefly a few years ago. I don't think she's right for me, but she is a great girl."

Taylor wasn't sure what to make of that. "Well, go out and have a good time. You never do know."

He nodded. "We can go out and have a good time as friends and then I can tell my mother we tried, and it wasn't meant to be."

Taylor laughed. "You seem very sure of that. What if the spark reignites?"

This time, it was Blake's turn to laugh. "I don't see that happening. What about you? Are you dating anyone yet?"

"Me? No. I really haven't met anyone yet here. Other than people at work." Blake was the only person she had any interest in dating. Which was impossible, of course. She probably should get out there and meet more people so she could stop thinking about her boss all the time. She sighed and reached for another slice of pizza.

The TV was on, though they hadn't been paying much attention to it. A preview of the next movie flashed across the screen. It was the old Phantom of the Opera, starring Lon Chaney.

"Have you seen that movie?" Taylor asked.

Blake glanced at the TV. "No. That's the one we won trivia on, though. I wonder how scary it really is? I'm somewhat skeptical."

Taylor laughed. "Me too. I can't imagine it's worse than The Exorcist or Texas Chainsaw Massacre. I mean, they did make a musical of it, after all."

"Maybe we should watch it and see? Unless you have other plans?"

"No plans. Just hanging with Patricia all weekend. We could watch it. I am curious now too."

"I think I need more pizza. I'll grab the box." Blake stood and went to the kitchen.

"Good idea. We can stress eat as we watch," Taylor said.

He set the box down on the coffee table and they both helped themselves to another slice and settled in to watch the movie. Taylor was very aware that Blake was sitting just inches away from her on the sofa. The temptation to lean into him was strong, but of course she couldn't do that. She tried to focus on the movie instead.

They managed to finish the rest of the pizza as they watched the movie, and when it ended, Blake turned to her. "So what did you think?"

"It was good. But definitely not as scary as The Exorcist—and I've never watched Texas Chainsaw Massacre. It sounds too gory for me."

"Agreed." Blake glanced at his watch as Patricia got up and walked toward the door.

"I think someone needs to go out," Taylor said. She stood and took the empty pizza box and their plates into the kitchen.

"I should probably get going." Blake walked over to the door.

"Thanks so much for coming by to check on us, and for the pizza." She grabbed Patricia's leash and opened the door.

He held her gaze for a long moment before saying, "It was nothing. This was fun. Thanks for hanging out with me."

Taylor was tempted to say 'anytime', but thought better of it and walked outside. Blake followed and took a step toward his Jeep. "Enjoy the rest of your weekend. I'll see you on Monday."

CHAPTER 32

"I hate Wesley Stevens!" Victoria stormed into the office and dramatically slammed her purse down on her desk. She flopped into her chair and sighed with frustration.

Patricia had been peacefully sleeping by Taylor's feet and jumped at the sudden loudness.

It was Friday morning and Patricia was spending the whole day in the office before they went to meet her father at a quarter to five when his ferry arrived. Taylor brought Patricia in for half days until yesterday, and she'd adjusted faster than expected. She liked being around people and pretty much stayed by Taylor's side all day.

Taylor had been a little nervous when Patricia met Richard as she wasn't sure how that would go, but Richard was very mellow and just sniffed at her. Patricia kept her distance from him for the first few days, but now she seemed a little more comfortable around the other dog.

Taylor could tell Victoria wanted to talk about whatever was bothering her.

"What happened? Did you see him?"

"Our waitress from The Gaslight told us that he's been going into The Corner Table a few mornings a week for coffee and a pastry to go. I've been there every morning this week, waiting."

"And he never showed up?"

Victoria stood and paced around her desk. "Oh, he showed! He came in this morning, got his coffee and a muffin and on his way out, I tried to talk to him. He remembered me from the last time I got his picture with Bella. He looked me right in the eye and said he would never in a million years say a thing to me. And then he stomped off before I could even get a single shot. I was in shock, so my reflexes were slow. I wouldn't have gotten a good shot anyway as it would have been of his back. It's just such a disappointment. I really thought I could get him to talk to me. But he never gave me a chance."

Taylor wondered if he might have been more receptive if she hadn't taken those other photos and been so sneaky about it. But there didn't seem to be any point of mentioning that.

"That's too bad. I'm sorry it didn't work out."

Victoria had calmed down some, now that she'd paced her frustration away. "Oh it's fine. I just needed to vent. I'm done chasing celebrities. I'm going to focus on more important stories now."

"Good idea."

The rest of the day flew by and soon it was four thirty

and time to head to the ferry to meet her father. Blake walked through the office and looked to be in a great mood.

"Hey everyone. Emily just set a sales record and we've had our best ad sales month ever. First round of drinks is on me at the B-Ack Yard BBQ."

"That's fantastic. I'm ready for a cold one," Joe said.

"I'm more than ready. And Wesley Stevens had better hope he doesn't run into me again," Victoria said. So, clearly, she wasn't completely over it.

"Are you coming, Taylor?" Blake asked as he reached her desk. Richard was right behind him and stopped to rub noses with Patricia, who allowed it.

"No, it sounds fun, though. I'm off to meet my dad at the ferry."

"Oh, that's right. Is it his first time here on Nantucket?"

She nodded. "Yes, so we'll be playing tourist all weekend."

"That will be fun. Are you taking him to the Whaling Museum?"

"Yes, that will be our first stop tomorrow. He's a history buff, so I think he'll love it."

"Alright, we're off. See you on Monday, then."

Taylor watched them go and felt a pang that she was missing out. But she knew there would be many more opportunities for after-work drinks. And she was excited to show her father around Nantucket.

"Come on, Patricia."

.   .   .

Taylor had a fun time showing her father some of her favorite places on Nantucket. She and Patricia had met him on the wharf the night before when his ferry arrived. It had been a long day of driving for him. He'd parked his car in a lot in Hyannis and took the fast ferry over. He'd loved the ferry ride.

"It went by in a flash. Hardly an hour. Seemed like we'd just left Hyannis harbor and next thing I knew, we could see Nantucket in the distance. Nice smooth ride, too."

Taylor knew her father would be tired from the day of travel, so she'd made him a home-cooked meal, one of his favorites, a lasagna with meatballs. They'd relaxed at home over dinner and went for a long walk with Patricia, who her father had instantly fallen in love with.

She took him to The Corner Table the next morning for a breakfast treat. She knew her father loved baked goods, and they had a great selection. They lingered over coffee and scones before walking the short distance to the Whaling Museum and spent several hours there. Her father was fascinated by it, as she'd anticipated.

He'd never been much of a shopper, but they strolled around for a bit and popped into some art galleries to see the local artwork. Her dad had taken up painting as a hobby and always enjoyed seeing what other artists had created. She was impressed to see that one of the galleries they stopped into had some of Kristen Hodges' paintings displayed.

"That's Abby's sister," she said as she pointed them out to her father.

"Those are really lovely. She has a gift."

They spent the rest of the afternoon back at the cottage and took Patricia for another long walk.

When dinner time rolled around, Taylor offered her father a choice.

"What do you feel like doing for dinner? We could go fancy and go to one of the restaurants downtown or, if you want something more casual but still really good, we could go to Millie's. It's mostly Mexican but they have great seafood dishes, too."

Her father didn't hesitate. "We're not much into fancy in Vermont. Millie's sounds more up my alley."

She grinned. "It's more my speed, too. And the food is really good."

She filled Patricia's bowls with fresh food and water and they headed off to Millie's a little after six.

It was a Saturday night, and nice weather, so Millie's was busy, but they didn't have to wait long for a table. The hostess led them upstairs and to a table for two near a window. Her father glanced out the window as they sat.

"Well, that's impressive. I hope the food is as good as the view." They could see the sandy beach and dunes and white-tipped waves of the ocean beyond.

"It is," Taylor assured him.

When their server came, they both ordered frozen raspberry margaritas and fresh guacamole and chips to start. She talked him into splitting two orders of tacos with her, one fish, and one scallop and bacon. "You need to try both, and I can never decide. But, trust me on this."

Her father laughed. "It all sounds good to me."

Everything was delicious and her father couldn't decide which taco he preferred. "Glad you talked me into this. We don't have anything like this in Vermont. We do have the best maple syrup you'll ever have, though. That reminds me—I have a half-gallon of the stuff in my suitcase for you. Don't let me forget to give it to you."

"Thank you. I won't. I'll make us pancakes tomorrow for breakfast, so we'll need it."

Taylor froze as she spotted two familiar faces coming their way—Blake and Andi. They were both smiling and laughing, and it looked like they were having a marvelous time on their date. She'd known it was tonight, but Blake hadn't mentioned where they were going. Of course, it had to be where she and her father decided to go. Blake stopped short when he saw her.

"Taylor. Nice to see you. This must be your father?"

Her dad looked surprised at being recognized. Taylor quickly introduced them. "Dad, this is Blake, my boss at the paper and his friend, Andi." She wasn't sure how else to describe her and hoped friend was appropriate.

"Nice to meet you," Andi said politely.

Blake shook his hand. "A pleasure to meet you. I know Taylor was looking forward to your visit."

Her father smiled. "It's my first time on Nantucket. We went to the Whaling Museum today. Fantastic place."

"It's one of my favorite places, too. Well, enjoy the rest of your visit."

"See you on Monday," Taylor added.

Once they were gone, her father commented, "He seems like a nice fellow. That his girlfriend?"

"He is nice. And I don't know. I hope not," Taylor admitted.

Her father looked sympathetic. "Do I detect some kind of interest there?"

"Maybe. We've been hanging out together some after work, but just as friends. We play trivia every week with a group of people, mostly others in the office. It's a lot of fun. I just haven't met anyone else yet that I'm interested in."

"Well, might be for the best. Could get messy if you dated and things didn't work—with him being your direct boss. Might be different if you reported to someone else, maybe. Lots of people meet at work. That's how your mother and I met. We started work at the same company a week apart."

"That's right. I forgot about that. But you were co-workers, so that was different."

"Right. So, I think you mentioned something to me about a great place to get ice cream on Nantucket? How about we go get a scoop?"

Taylor smiled. "Sure, Dad. That's a great idea."

CHAPTER 33

"What can I do to help?" Mark asked. He was leaning against the kitchen island, watching Marley work. It was Saturday night, and she was having her first dinner party at the new house, and she wanted everything to be perfect. She was almost ready—with about ten minutes to spare before people started arriving. She knew Lisa and Rhett would probably be the first to arrive and would be right on time.

"I think I'm actually just about done. You could open a bottle of cabernet and pour us both a glass if you like?" Marley took a peek in the oven. She'd made a rich chicken stew, a recipe her kids had always loved, and she knew it was a safe one for a dinner party. She planned to serve it with creamy mashed potatoes, which were done and keeping warm next to the stew, and a big salad.

She'd put together a cheese tray with an assortment of different cheeses that had looked intriguing at the market, some crisp crackers and a small bowl of salted nuts, all perfect for nibbling while they had a glass of wine or a cocktail before dinner.

"I can do that." Mark found a good bottle of cabernet from her wine refrigerator, opened it and poured them each a glass. "Cheers!" He waited for her to lift her glass so they could tap them together. "Don't worry about a thing. They will love it all. Whatever is in the oven smells great." He leaned over and gave her a quick kiss before they were interrupted by the doorbell. Things were going well with Mark and she was glad that he was there early with her.

Marley opened the door and Lisa and Rhett were there and Paige and her boyfriend, Peter Bradford, were walking up behind them. As they stepped inside, Marley saw another car pull into the driveway. Sue and her husband Curtis had arrived.

Once everyone had a glass of wine, or in Curt's case, a bottle of beer, they all gathered around the island and chatted as they snacked on the appetizers. When they were ready to sit down to dinner, Mark helped by carrying in bowls of stew as Marley ladled them out. The conversation was lively around the dinner table and Marley realized how much she had missed doing this— having people over for dinner.

"We need to do this more often," she said at one point.

Rhett laughed. "Anytime, we'll gladly be here."

Lisa agreed. "We really do need to do this more often. We can all take turns hosting. It's much more fun than going to a restaurant and we can relax and take our time."

"How is it going with the new bakers?" Marley asked. She was curious to see how that was working out for Lisa.

"It was hard to let go of it. I was a nervous wreck this week, especially the first few days, but so far, it's going smoothly. And I think it should work out well once we boost the ad spending a little. At least I hope it will." She still seemed a little nervous at the idea of scaling the business. Marley had a good feeling about it, though.

"I think you will be very pleasantly surprised by what's possible now that you've added the ability to meet a higher demand." She smiled. "Pretty soon everyone will know about your lobster quiches!"

Lisa smiled. "I'm still surprised by how popular they seem to be. And very grateful. What about you—are you still busy with new assignments since the conference you and Frank went to?"

Marley nodded. "Yes, and I just got another referral this week from someone I talked with that knew someone who needed some marketing help.

"That's great. How's your ex doing? Did he ever get back with his young girlfriend?" Lisa asked.

"No. But my daughter said he's dating someone closer to his age now, and seems to be happy, so that's a good thing." It was someone that Frank had once worked with and left to start her own services company, so they had a lot in common and her daughter seemed to like her. Marley was happy for him.

"Whatever happened to those twins that stole from your restaurant?" Sue asked Rhett.

"That actually just resolved this week. They avoided jail time, as it was a first offense for both of them. First time they got caught, that is. The judge sentenced them to six months of community service and they both have to pay a hefty fine, to me for reimbursement of what they stole. So, I'm sure they would disagree, but I think it worked out the way that it should. I'm happy with it."

"And it will go on their record," Lisa added. "So it won't be easy for them to get another restaurant job and pull that same nonsense again."

"Good. Maybe they've learned their lesson," Marley said.

Rhett looked thoughtful. "I hope so, but I'm not so sure. Neither one of them had one bit of remorse. They were only sorry that they got caught. The sense of entitlement was astounding."

Lisa smiled. "Maybe they will find a more legal way to channel their entrepreneurial abilities."

Rhett laughed at that. "I hope so. Maybe they will. They were likable kids. I hope they will learn from this."

Later that evening, once everyone had gone home and the kitchen was all cleaned up, Marley and Mark curled up on the living room sofa to watch a little television before bed.

"I think that was a good night. Everyone seemed to have fun," Mark said.

"It was really my idea of a perfect night. Good

friends, good food and we didn't have to leave the house. It doesn't get much better than that."

Mark laughed, then leaned over and kissed her. "You're right. It doesn't get much better than this."

Marley sighed with happiness. She had everything she needed. Things were going great with Mark and she had made some good friends. Overall, she couldn't be happier with how things had turned out for her on Nantucket. And once he'd gotten over the initial rejection, Mark had understood that her not wanting to get married had nothing to do with him. They were in a good place and Marley just wanted to freeze this moment in time and keep things the way they were for as long as possible.

CHAPTER 34

The next morning, as promised, Taylor made pancakes from scratch and they used the real maple syrup her father brought for her.

"This came from a farm right up the road. When you're running low, let me know and I'll get some more for you."

Taylor laughed. "Thank you. But I think this will hold me for a while." Her last jug of syrup had lasted several years.

She and Patricia drove her father to the wharf so he could catch the ten thirty ferry back to Hyannis as he still had a good five or six-hour drive home after that, depending on what kind of traffic he hit when he went through Boston.

"Okay, your turn to come see me next," her father teased as they waited for the signal to board.

"I will."

"Seriously, though, I had a great time, honey. And

don't worry about that boss of yours. As your mother used to say, and I agree with this, if it's meant to be, it will happen."

"Thanks, Dad." She gave him a big hug and watched as they gave the signal to board and her father stepped forward. She and Patricia waited on the wharf and watched as the boat loaded everyone on and slowly pulled away from the pier. They drove home and went back inside and the cottage felt suddenly empty and quiet without the energy of her father. She sighed, grateful that Patricia was there.

She flopped onto the sofa and Patricia followed and settled into her dog bed. Taylor pulled a cozy fleece throw around her and clicked on the TV and found the Hallmark channel. It was exactly what she needed, a feel-good Christmas movie to take her mind off feeling suddenly very alone, with no family nearby and just a sweet dog for company.

By the time the movie ended, she was herself again, and was just happy for the fun weekend with her father. She also told herself that she needed to get over Blake, as it looked like he may have moved on with Andi. They looked good together, and happy. Eventually, she would find that, too.

CHAPTER 35

"Coffee? We early birds need to stick together," Blake's father said as Taylor and Patricia walked into the office on Monday morning.

Taylor laughed. "Yes, please." It was a quarter past eight and they were the only ones in the office so far, which was normal. Taylor was an early riser too, and she liked getting into the office early, before it got busy. She liked settling in at her desk and going through her email while enjoying her morning coffee.

"How was your weekend?" She asked.

"Oh, it was pretty uneventful. Did a little fishing, didn't catch anything but had a fantastic time trying. What about you?"

"It was a fun weekend. My father was in town, and it was his first time here, so we played tourist."

"Good, I hope he'll come back?"

"I'm sure he will. But he said it's my turn to head up to visit him next time. He's in central Vermont."

"That's beautiful country up there. We used to head up that way to go skiing at Killington. Is he near there?"

"He's not too far from there."

"All right, young lady, I won't keep you. Have a good Monday." He bent down and gave Patricia a scratch behind her ears before taking his coffee and heading back to his office. Taylor did the same and settled at her desk. Patricia flopped down by her feet as she turned on her computer.

A half hour later, as she was about to go for more coffee, a very quiet, red-eyed Victoria came in and sat at her desk without saying a word. It was so unlike her that Taylor wasn't sure what to do. She got up and refilled her coffee mug and on the way back saw that Victoria was staring at her computer screen, but it hadn't powered on yet. Something was not right with her.

Taylor sat down and gently asked, "How was your weekend?" She wasn't sure what to say, but felt like she had to say something.

Victoria turned around slowly and her face was paler than Taylor had ever seen it. Usually she had lots of natural color and light makeup. Today her eyes were bare and there were dark shadows and not a hint of color anywhere. She looked like she was utterly cried out.

"Todd broke up with me yesterday. It still doesn't seem real."

"Oh no! I'm so sorry." And surprised. They'd been engaged and discussing their wedding and things had seemed fine when Taylor had seen them together. But she realized she didn't know Todd at all, and she barely knew Victoria.

"I was completely blind-sided. We've been together for so long. I just—I just didn't expect this."

Taylor was quiet and waited for her to go on.

"He's not leaving me for someone else, so that's one good thing. I don't think I could have handled that. But this isn't much better. He's moving to Alaska!"

"Alaska? Why?"

"Right, that's what I said. Why would anyone do that? He said he's sick of real estate and wants to chase his dream, which is apparently bass fishing. He said Alaska has the best fishing and hunting in the US."

"He's a hunter too?"

"No! I don't think he's ever hunted in his life. But he thinks he can have a career as a bass fisherman. I asked why couldn't he do that here? Nantucket has bass, I think?"

"They do. I see them at Trattel's market, local bass fish."

"I guess it's not the same as Alaska. He wants a change. And he said he's not ready to get married, to anyone. And that he should have ended things a long time ago, but getting engaged was just what everyone expected. And he's always done that. Until now."

"I'm so sorry, Victoria. Do you think it might just be a phase he's going through? Maybe something he needs to get out of his system and then he'll come back?"

Victoria sat up straight and a bit of color came back

to her cheeks, along with her attitude. "Maybe, but if he does come back, it won't be to me. I told him if he does this, if he leaves and goes to Alaska, that we are done. Totally done. And he said fine. I don't think he has any interest in making this work in the future."

"Will you stay here? Or go back to the Herald?" Taylor knew the main reason she'd moved home was for Todd, since he worked on Nantucket in the family real estate business.

"I'm not sure. I haven't thought that far ahead, to be honest. I do like it here. More than I expected, and my family is here. They are completely and totally horrified by his behavior. So, I'm glad to have their support right now."

"I'm glad you have it, too. And you have friends here too."

Victoria nodded. "Most of my old friends have moved off-island, but I'm glad to have you all. It was fun going out Friday night—and now I know why Todd was too busy to meet us out like he usually did. We had a good time without him, though. Just about everyone from the paper went—we missed you. Did you have a good weekend with your father?"

"We did, thanks. I'm glad you had fun with everyone on Friday. I was sorry to miss that. But I know there will be lots of other nights out. I know you're not keen on trivia, but you might want to join us sometime. We have a good group that goes. It might be fun for you."

"Maybe I will. Let me know next time you all go."

"I will, and if I can do anything to help, let me know. I'm so sorry, Victoria."

She sighed. "Thanks. I'll be okay. It's just a big shock, you know. It hasn't really hit me fully yet."

LATER THAT WEEK, WHEN THEY WENT TO TRIVIA, Victoria joined them and Taylor was glad to see that she seemed to have a good time. Victoria could be a lot of fun and she didn't take herself seriously when it came to trivia. Angela and Philippe joined them again and while they didn't win, thanks to Victoria knowing the answer to the final question, which was something to do with weddings, they came in second place, which meant a gift card they could put toward their next visit.

"At least my almost wedding helped with trivia—who knew?" She joked. Once the initial shock wore off, she'd accepted that her engagement with Todd was over and she shared that he was moving to Alaska the next week.

"It's crazy, but I guess it's good that if he's going he just does it, instead of hanging around talking about it. Then we can both move on." She'd thrown herself into her work and was keeping busy, which Taylor thought was a good thing. She didn't know how well she would have handled a breakup like that, especially when there were no warning signs.

Once again, Blake sat next to her and they laughed and joked all night as they played trivia. It was her favorite night, and she looked forward to it all week. But she knew she should get out there and meet more people. But she didn't feel in a hurry to do that. She just wasn't anxious to go on a date with anyone other than Blake.

CHAPTER 36

Friday morning around nine thirty, Blake's father wandered into his office, holding his coffee mug, as usual. Blake left his door open so people knew it was okay to walk in. He looked up and smiled when he saw it was his father.

"Hey, Dad."

"You busy? Thought I'd drop in and chat for a few minutes." His father usually popped into his office at least once each day to catch up. Blake welcomed the break.

"Perfect timing, actually. I just finished editing Taylor's latest piece." His office had floor to ceiling windows that looked out over the newsroom. He smiled when he saw Taylor and Victoria having a lively discussion while Joe looked on.

"You like her."

His father had noticed him watching Taylor as she laughed at something Victoria said.

"I do. She's a great girl."

His father came in and sat in the chair opposite Blake's desk. He lifted his mug and sipped his coffee. Richard walked over and rested his head on his dad's knee. He patted the dog and scratched behind his ears.

"Did you know that your mother once worked for me? That's how we met. The summer that she answered phones here at the front desk."

Blake smiled. He'd heard the story many times.

"Dad, things were different then. It's just not a good idea these days."

His father was quiet for a moment and looked out into the newsroom, where Taylor and Victoria were still chatting with Joe.

"How long has Joe worked here?"

The question took Blake by surprise. "Close to twenty years I think."

"And has his job changed much in that time?"

"Sure, he's taken on bigger, more important stories."

His father looked thoughtful. "Maybe he's ready to take on even more. I have an idea, that could offer a solution to your current issue too."

He told him what he had in mind, and Blake began to feel a glimmer of hope. If Joe was on board, it could be very good for both of them.

THE FOLLOWING MONDAY, TAYLOR SENSED A CHANGE IN the air. The feeling started when Joe was called into Blake's office and spent over an hour there with Blake and his father. When Joe went back to his desk, he was very quiet but seemed somewhat excited too, and Taylor guessed he was hard at work on a new story. Maybe something big and involved. She wondered what it might be, but figured they'd find out soon enough.

The feeling that something was about to shift persisted all week. Victoria noticed it too, but neither one of them had any idea what was going on. Joe met with Blake and his father several more times over the next few days. Thursday morning, Blake came out into the newsroom and there was a sense of excitement about him. Joe was sitting on the edge of his seat and looked excited, too.

Blake looked around the newsroom. "Victoria and Taylor, I have something exciting to announce. We've made a management change and have decided to promote Joe to a new role. We think he has a lot to offer to both of you, given his many years, just over twenty now, with the paper. So, effective immediately, you will both be reporting to Joe."

Victoria's jaw dropped. "Are you leaving?"

Taylor's heart sank as she waited for him to answer. She'd never imagined that Blake would leave. And she wasn't sure how she felt about reporting to Joe. She liked Joe, but he wasn't Blake.

Blake smiled. "I'm not going anywhere. We've just decided that this makes sense. I used to write an opinion piece and haven't done that in months, so I'm going to start that up again and take on some other projects and of course I'll be here to help too, if anyone needs it. But, going forward, Joe will be your boss." He grinned. "I'll just be that co-worker that nags you to go to trivia or after-work drinks."

Victoria smiled. "Well, that's a relief. I've had enough change lately. Glad you're not going anywhere." She turned to Joe. "Congratulations, Joe. I look forward to you teaching me all of your secrets."

Joe laughed. "I'm looking forward to it, too. I think I have some things I could help you both with."

"Congratulations, Joe," Taylor offered. She still wasn't sure how she felt about this, but she could see he was excited and she'd benefited when he took her along on his interview. She knew she had a lot more to learn.

They all went to trivia that night after work. Taylor ran Patricia home first and got her settled, then drove back and walked over with everyone. Both Joe and Blake were in celebratory moods. They played horribly, and didn't come close to winning, but no one cared. They still had a good time.

Victoria didn't join them as she had a previously scheduled hair appointment. On the walk back to the office, when they reached the entrance and Taylor was about to walk back to her car, Blake surprised her by inviting her in.

"Do you have a minute to come inside? There's something I want to talk to you about and I'd also love to have you take a look at the kitchen and give me your opinion. If you're not in a hurry?" He seemed a little nervous, which she found curious.

"Sure, I can come up for a minute."

She followed him upstairs and was surprised by how

big his place was. She'd pictured it like a small apartment, but it was more loft-like and spacious. He gave her the tour and took her upstairs, where he had two big bedrooms and a bathroom. It was dark out, but she imagined that during the day his views were incredible of the harbor. They went back downstairs to the kitchen.

"So, what do you think?" Blake asked.

"I love it. I could totally see you flip-flopping the levels and putting the kitchen and living room upstairs. I think that's a great idea."

"Good. I think I am going to get going on that soon. But that's not the main reason I wanted to talk to you."

"Oh? What is it?"

Blake took a step closer and held her gaze for a moment, and her pulse picked up. The air shifted. At least to her it did. Was she imagining it?

"So, what do you think of the management change and reporting to Joe now? I think it will be a good thing."

"It was a surprise. But I think it should be fine. I like Joe and I think I can learn a lot from him. I liked reporting to you too, though," she admitted.

He smiled. "I'm glad to hear that. There's another advantage though of you reporting to Joe instead of me."

"What's that?"

"Well, if I'm not your direct boss, if I'm just a co-worker, maybe you'd consider saying yes if I asked you on a date? If that's ever crossed your mind?"

She was shocked speechless, so he kept talking. "Or if not, if I've totally misread this, we can forget this conversation ever happened."

She smiled and took a step closer to him. "You didn't misread it."

A warmth and relief came into his eyes. "Good! You had me worried for a moment. So, are you up for dinner sometime this weekend?"

"Yes."

"There's one other thing. Something I've been wanting to do for a long time." He leaned forward and her heart raced as he touched his lips against hers. She'd been wanting this for so long, too. His kiss was better than she'd imagined, and she didn't want it to stop. But eventually it did. They both just stared at each other, caught up in the wonder of having something they both wanted finally coming to fruition.

"I'll walk you downstairs."

He walked her to her car, and they kissed again and made plans to have dinner the next night. Taylor drove home, took Patricia for a quick walk outside and then drifted into sleep, looking forward to her first real date with Blake.

EPILOGUE

"Bring it here," Taylor told Abby. "Then no matter what the result is, we'll either be celebrating or supporting you."

"Are you sure? I don't want to ruin your appetizer party. Maybe I should just stay home," Abby said.

"Don't be ridiculous. It's a small group and everyone there loves you. Well, except for Victoria, but she just doesn't know you yet and I can guarantee she will love the drama of this."

Abby laughed. "Okay, you've convinced me. I just don't want to get my hopes up. I'm supposed to have my first treatment next week and I'm not really sure I'm late. I did spot a little, so I'm pretty sure it's going to be negative."

"It might be. Stop at CVS on your way and take the

test when you get here. And either way we are going to have fun."

"Okay. I'm on my way. I just took my brownies out of the oven and Jeff is all set to watch Natalie."

"Perfect, I'll see you soon, then."

It was a Tuesday night. The needlepoint class was over, so Taylor thought it would be a good night to have everyone over, as both Abby and Beth were used to going out on a Tuesday night. Kate and Kristen were also coming, as well as Angela, who Taylor had become good friends with and saw every week at trivia. And Victoria had also become a good friend.

Now that she and Todd had broken up, she had opened up to Taylor, and they often went out to dinner or drinks, too. And she had sworn off dating for at least a year. Though Taylor suspected she wouldn't wait that long.

Everyone was bringing their favorite appetizer and Taylor had stocked up on both red and white wine. She made sure to feed Patricia so she wouldn't be giving everyone those big, sad looks as they ate. She opened the oven and checked on the grilled cheese and lobster mini-sandwiches that she'd made. They looked nice and golden, so she turned off the heat and pulled the tray out of the oven and covered it with aluminum foil so it would stay warm.

It was a recipe that she'd tried for the first time, and she hoped that everyone would like it. It looked good—she'd sliced a crusty baguette, buttered both sides and toasted them lightly in a pan, then added a slice of nutty but mellow Gruyère cheese and a scoop of chopped sweet lobster, then topped with another slice of cheese and a baguette slice. She couldn't wait to try one.

Within a few minutes, people started arriving. Beth and Kate were first, followed by Abby, Angela, Victoria and lastly, Kristen. Beth brought a homemade fig, goat cheese and prosciutto pizza that she'd cut into small pieces. Angela made hot spiced mixed nuts, Kate brought salsa, guacamole and chips, Kristen made a big Caesar salad, and Victoria brought some cheese and crackers. Abby walked in with her still-warm brownies and a paper bag from CVS. Taylor showed her where the bathroom was. A moment later, she was back.

"Okay, it's done. In five minutes, I'll go see what my fate is. I don't want to say anything until then."

Taylor gave her a hug. "That's fine. Whatever the results are, we're here for you. Are you ready for a glass of wine?"

Abby hesitated. "Yes, but I should probably wait. I'll have water for now."

"Oh, of course. I have some flavored seltzer water, if you want that. Black Cherry. It's good."

"That's perfect, thanks."

Taylor poured it into a dark wine glass, so no one would notice what Abby was or wasn't drinking. She had a feeling her friend wasn't ready for questions just yet.

Everyone set their food either on Taylor's kitchen counter or island and they helped themselves to wine and snacks. She took the tin foil off of the lobster grilled cheeses and everyone oohed and aahed over them. The buttery toasted bread, melty cheese and fresh sweet lobster were a great combination.

"Taylor, these are so good. My mother would love them!" Kate said.

"She totally would," Kristen agreed. "We should suggest them for her Fourth of July party."

Taylor noticed after a few minutes that Abby slipped away to the bathroom. She crossed her fingers and wished for good luck for her friend.

"So, Taylor, how are things going with Blake?" Beth asked. She'd known about Taylor's crush from the needle-point class and had been thrilled like everyone else when they started dating.

"It's going really well. We've been officially dating now, ever since he promoted Joe. He said it was his father's idea because Blake was uncomfortable about asking me out while I still reported to him. I didn't feel right about that either."

"It's worked out well, too," Victoria said. "Joe knows a lot and I've already learned a lot from him now that he's more involved in the day-to-day."

Taylor nodded. "I have too. And I think Blake is happier focusing on other stuff."

"Philippe is glad that he started up his column again," Angela added. "He's a really good writer."

"He is," Taylor agreed. She'd been impressed by Blake's thoughtful opinion pieces, where he looked at all sides of an issue. He'd admitted that he'd missed doing projects like that. So, even though he'd wanted to shift the reporting so they could date, it was overall a better move for the business too—for Joe's and for Blake's strengths.

And she was really happy with how things were going. It was easy with Blake. They got along well and shared so many similar interests. And she had to laugh—even their dogs got along. Richard had taken to wandering out of Blake's office mid-day and taking his afternoon nap next to Patricia, so Taylor had two dogs at her feet. But she didn't mind. She was glad they got along.

Abby came out of the bathroom holding the pregnancy stick and wearing a dazed grin. "You guys, I have the craziest news. It looks like I'm pregnant. I won't have to start fertility treatments next week after all!"

Everyone rushed over to give her a hug and offer congratulations.

"Did you feel like you might be pregnant? Or were you just late?" Kristen asked.

"A little of both. I sort of recognized the feelings this time. My breasts have been tender and I've been tired, but I spotted a little so I didn't want to get my hopes up. I have to go call Jeff." She went outside to make the call.

"I am so happy for her," Kate said.

"Me too. I'm so glad this test wasn't negative," Taylor said.

"She's probably calling our mother after Jeff," Kristen said. "She's going to be thrilled."

"I'm going to miss our Tuesday nights at needlepoint," Beth said. Taylor had enjoyed seeing her and Abby every week, too.

"There's an advanced class. We could think about

doing that. Or you could always come to trivia on Thursday nights. The more the merrier. We have Victoria going now."

Victoria laughed. "They wore me down. It is fun though, just to be out with everyone. It's something to do."

"That could be fun. Maybe I could get Chase to do it, too. Abby might not feel up to another round of needlepoint. I think I remember that she was exhausted during her first trimester with Natalie."

"I was." Abby was back and heard the tail end of what Beth had said. "I think you should count me out for more needlepoint. It was fun, but I don't want to over commit when I don't know how I'll be feeling. Beth, you should do trivia."

Beth laughed. "Okay, you've talked me into it. I'll check with Chase and see what he thinks."

"What did Jeff say? Is he so excited?" Taylor asked.

Abby's eyes glowed with happiness. "Yes, we both are. I called my mother too and gave her the good news. She's thrilled."

Taylor looked around the room and felt a wave of happiness. She was excited for her best friend and content to be surrounded by friends in her new home. Her job was going well and things with Blake were wonderful.

"So, Taylor, are you glad you moved to Nantucket?" Victoria asked as she reached for a brownie.

Taylor smiled. "More than I ever imagined that I would be."

THANK YOU SO MUCH FOR READING! I HOPE YOU ENJOYED this story. If you'd like to be notified about the next book in this series and other new releases, please join my mailing list, or visit my web site, www.pamelakelley.com.

I'd also like to invite you to join my Pamela Kelley Facebook Reader Group, which is such a fun, happy, feel-good place where we talk about books, pets, food and where I often seek your input on covers, character names, book titles....join the fun today.

If you like mystery/suspense, you might enjoy a recent new release, book one in a new series set in my hometown of Plymouth. Plymouth Undercover is a blend of women's fiction and mystery.

Thanks so much for reading!!!

XOXO Pam

Made in the USA
Las Vegas, NV
30 September 2021